Rigoberta Menchú

Women Changing the World

Aung San Suu Kyi
Standing Up for Democracy in Burma

Rigoberta Menchú
Defending Human Rights in Guatemala

Máiread Corrigan and Betty Williams
Making Peace in Northern Ireland

Advisory Board for Women Changing the World

Rigoberta Menchú

Defending Human Rights in Guatemala

Michael Silverstone

The Feminist Press
at The City University of New York

Published by The Feminist Press at The City University of New York
City College, Wingate Hall, Convent Avenue at 138th Street, New York, NY 10031
www.feministpress.org

First edition, 1999

Library of Congress Cataloging-in-Publication Data

Silverstone, Michael.
    Rigoberta Menchú: defending human rights in Guatemala / Michael Silverstone.
      p.. cm. — (Women changing the world)
    Includes bibliographical references (p.   ) and index.
    ISBN 1-55861-198-3 (lb. hc). ISBN 1-55861-199-1 (pb.).
     1. Menchú, Rigoberta—Juvenile literature. 2. Quiché women—Biography—Juvenile literature.
3. Human rights workers—Guatemala—Biography—Juvenile literature.
4. Mayas—civil rights—Juvenile literature. 5. Guatemala—Ethnic relations—Juvenile literature.
I. Title. II. Series.
F1465.2.Q5M3884 1999
972.81'00497415—dc21   98-41996
                                                    CIP
                                                       AC

The Feminist Press is grateful to the Ford Foundation for their generous support of our work. The Feminist Press is also grateful to Jane S. Gould, Johnetta B. Cole, William L. Hedges, Florence Howe, Caroline Urvater, Genevieve Vaughn, Susan Weiler and Lynn Gernert, Patricia Wentworth and Mark Fagan, and Joanna Markell for their generosity in supporting this publication.

Printed on acid-free paper by RR Donnelley & Sons

Manufactured in Mexico

05   04   03   02   01   00   99   5   4   3   2   1

CONTENTS

WHAT DOES IT TAKE TO CHANGE THE WORLD?

Maybe this question sounds overwhelming. However, people who become leaders have all had to ask themselves this question at some point. They started finding answers by choosing how they would lead their lives every day and by creating their own opportunities to make a difference in the world. The anthropologist Margaret Mead said, "Never doubt that a small group of thoughtful, committed citizens can change the world; indeed it's the only thing that ever has." So let's look at some of the qualities possessed by people who are determined to change the world.

First, it takes vision. The great stateswoman and humanitarian Eleanor Roosevelt said, "You must do the thing you think you cannot do." People who change the world have the ability to see what is wrong in their society. They also have the ability to imagine something new and better. They do not accept the way things *are*—the "status quo"— as the only way things *must be* or *can be*. It is this vision of an improved world that inspires others to join leaders in their efforts to make change. Leaders are not afraid to be different, and the fear of failure does not prevent them from trying to create a better world.

Second, it takes courage. Mary Frances Berry, former head of the U.S. Commission on Civil Rights, said, "The time when you need to do something is when no one else is willing to do it, when people are saying it can't be done." People who change the world know that courage means more than just saying what needs to be changed. It means deciding to be active in the effort to bring about change—no matter what it takes. They know they face numerous challenges: they may be criticized, made fun of, ignored, alienated from their friends and family, imprisoned, or even killed. But even though they may sometimes feel scared, they continue to pursue their vision of a better world.

Third, it takes dedication and patience. The Nobel Prize–winning scientist Marie Curie said, "One never notices what has been done; one can only see what remains to be done." People who change the world understand that change does not happen overnight. Changing the world is an ongoing process. They also know that while what they do is important, change depends on what others do as well. Their original vision may transform and evolve over time as it interacts with the visions of others and as circumstances change. And they know that the job is never finished. Each success brings a new challenge, and each failure yet another obstacle to overcome.

Finally, it takes inspiration. People who change the world find strength in the experiences and accomplishments of others who came before them. Sometimes these role models are family members or personal friends. Sometimes they are great women and men who have spoken out and written about their own struggles to change the world for the better. Reading books about these people—learning about their lives and reading their own words—can be a source of inspiration for future world-changers. For example, when I was young, someone gave me a book called *Girls' Stories of Great Women,* which provided me with ideas of what women had achieved in ways I had never dreamed of and in places that were very distant from my small town. It helped me to imagine what I could do with my life and to know that I myself could begin working toward my goals.

This series of books introduces us to women who have changed the world through their vision, courage, determination, and patience. Their stories reveal their struggles as world-changers against obstacles such as poverty, discrimination, violence, and injustice. Their stories also tell of their struggles as women to overcome the belief, which still exists in most societies, that girls are less capable than boys of achieving high goals, and that women are less likely than men to become leaders. These world-changing women often needed even more vision and courage than their male counterparts, because as women they faced greater discrimination and resistance. They certainly needed more determination and patience, because no matter how much they proved themselves, there were always people who were reluctant to take their leadership and their achievements seriously, simply because they were women.

These women and many others like them did not allow these challenges to stop them. As they fought on, they found inspiration in women as well as men—their own mothers and grandmothers, and the great women who had come before them. And now they themselves stand as an inspiration to young women and men all over the world.

The women whose lives are described in this series come from different countries around the world and represent a variety of cultures. Their stories offer insights into the lives of people in varying circumstances. In some ways, their lives may seem very different from the lives of most people in the United States. We can learn from these differences as well as from the things we have in common. Women often share similar problems and concerns about issues such as violence in their lives and in the world, or the kind of environment we are creating for the future. Further, the qualities that enable women to become leaders, and to make positive changes, are often the same worldwide.

The first set of books in this series tells the stories of four women who have won what might be called humanity's highest honor: the Nobel Peace Prize.

The Nobel Peace Prize recognizes leaders who try to improve their societies using peaceful means. These leaders have faced many different kinds of challenges and have responded to them in different ways. But one goal they all share is to promote "human rights"—the basic rights to which all human beings are entitled.

In 1948, the United Nations adopted the *Universal Declaration of Human Rights,* which outlines the rights of all people to freedom from slavery and torture, and to freedom of movement, speech, religion, and assembly, as well as rights of all people to social security, work, health, housing, education, culture, and citizenship. Further, it states that all people have the equal right to all these human rights, "without distinction of any kind such as race, color, sex, language . . . or other status."

In the United States, many of these ideas are not new to us. Some of them can be found in the first ten amendments to the U.S. Constitution, known as the Bill of Rights. Yet these ideals continually face many challenges, and they must be defended and expanded by every generation. They have been tested in this country, for example, by the Civil Rights Movement to end racial discrimination and the movement to bring about equal rights for women. They continue to be tested even today by various individuals and groups who are fighting for greater equality and justice.

All over the world, women and men work for and defend the common goal of human rights for all. In some places these rights are severely violated.

Tradition and prejudice as well as social, economic, and political interests often exclude women, in particular, from benefiting from these basic rights. Over the past decade, women around the world have been questioning why "women's rights" and women's lives have been deemed secondary to "human rights" and the lives of men. As a result, an international women's human rights movement has emerged, with support from organizations such as the Center for Women's Global Leadership, to challenge limited ideas about human rights and to alert all nations that "women's rights are human rights."

The following biography is the true story of a woman overcoming incredible obstacles—economic hardship, religious persecution, political oppression, and even the threat of violence and death—in order to peacefully achieve greater respect for human rights in her country. I am sure that you will find her story inspiring. I hope it also encourages you to join in the struggle to demand an end to all human rights violations—regardless of sex, race, class, or culture—throughout the world. And perhaps it will motivate you to become someone who just might change the world.

Charlotte Bunch
Founder and Executive Director
Center for Women's Global Leadership
Rutgers University

You can help to change the world now by establishing goals for yourself personally and by setting an example in how you live and work within your own family and community. You can speak out against unfairness and prejudice whenever you see it or hear it expressed by those around you. You can join an organization that is fighting for something you believe in, volunteer locally, or even start your own group in your school or neighborhood so that other people who share your beliefs can join you. Don't let anything or anyone limit your vision. Make your voice heard with confidence, strength, and dedication . . . and start changing the world today.

The time has come for dawn, for work to be completed, for those who nourish and sustain us to appear, the enlightened sons, the civilized people; the time has come for the appearance of humanity on the surface of the Earth.

—From the *Popol Vuh*, the sacred book of the Maya

Rigoberta Menchú Tum, winner of the 1992 Nobel Peace Prize.

Chapter 1

A BRAVE YOUNG GIRL

Deep in the mountains of Guatemala, a young girl named Rigoberta Menchú walked barefoot with her sister. It was 3 A.M., and the two girls advanced through the forest surrounded by darkness. The only light came from the moon shining through the palm leaves overhead and the glow of an *ocote*, a small torch made from a burning pine branch, which Rigoberta held in her hand.

The rain forest jungle was thick and the night air was cool in the altiplano, the Guatemalan highlands. Rigoberta and her sister were dressed for work in the fields in the only clothes they had. They wore long, beautifully embroidered skirts called *cortes* and loose-fitting, colorful, blouses called *huipils*, but these were not enough to keep them warm. The girls made their way through the forest, fighting off the chill by hurrying along. The workday started early and the fields were far away.

It was dangerous in the forest, and they knew this. In their village, they had heard frightening stories of bears, coyotes, and other wild animals attacking people. Rigoberta's sister was afraid. Somehow Rigoberta remained calm. If she heard a noise, she would stop to listen. Otherwise, she would tell her sister to keep walking. By sunrise, they had made their way safely through the forest and arrived at a field, where they joined other workers picking coffee beans.

From a very young age, the children in Rigoberta's family worked long days picking coffee, cotton, or other crops to help their family in their constant battle against hunger and poverty. In the Guatemalan countryside, life is so hard that nearly every person in every family has to work. Few children attend school, even when they are very young.

Rigoberta Menchú grew up in the 1960s in one of the most beautiful places in the world, a land of eternal spring, with lush rain forests, beautiful birds, and flowers all around her. This beauty, however, could not change the fact that life was harsh in the altiplano. Her childhood memories were not the happy ones of playing with friends. She recalls mostly hard work, sad and exhausted families, sick and hungry children, and many funerals—including funerals of her own friends and family members. She remembers telling herself, "This is the life I will lead too; having many children, and having them die." Throughout the Guatemalan countryside, this is the way many people had come to expect life to be.

Rigoberta was given no reason to expect anything different. Her family could not afford to send their children to school. She had grown up knowing hunger. Her childhood was not much different from those of countless others in her country who suffered over the centuries: working hard for very little money, denied education, land, and food, while a small group of wealthy landowners grew rich from their labor.

But this overwhelming difficulty all around her did not stop Rigoberta from moving toward the life she longed for, just as the darkness did not stop her from walking through the jungle.

If this poor, barefoot girl could have held her torch up to glimpse her own future, she would probably have been astonished by the vision of things she might never have imagined, or dared to predict, for herself:

She would see herself achieving her dream of learning to read and write—something very few children, especially girls, learned in her country.

She would see herself helping her village organize and defend itself against an army.

She would see herself go into hiding, hunted by soldiers in Guatemala City.

She would see herself crying at many funerals of people she loved dearly, but never allowing grief to thwart her efforts.

She would see herself using her education to educate others and using her eloquent speaking and writing abilities to reach beyond her village's isolation and communicate her people's experiences to the world.

She would see herself become a leader in an international effort to help preserve ancient cultures and overcome poverty and human rights abuses, in her own country and around the world, at a decisive moment in human history.

As the moon shone down on them, young Rigoberta simply and calmly put one foot in front of the other and helped her sister complete a difficult and necessary journey. In this moment, perhaps she could not imagine the amazing things that lay ahead of her. Yet even as a young girl, she was ready to face whatever came with vision, with a love for her people, and with courage.

Chapter 2
GROWN-UP AT AN EARLY AGE

Rigoberta Menchú Tum (her full name, like those of many Guatemalans includes her mother's family name) was born on January 9, 1959, in the village of Chimel, in the mountains of northwest Guatemala.

The Menchú family and their neighbors in Chimel led their lives according to traditions thousands of years old. Like half of the ten million people in Guatemala, the Menchús were descendants of the Mayan people.

In villages where Mayan languages are spoken, ceremonies and practices that can be traced back to ancient times are continued today. A lot of what we now know about Mayan culture was recorded in a book called the *Popol Vuh*, which describes the old legends, stories, and practices.

As in the old days, the people of the surviving mountain villages believe that one's first duty is to one's community. They also believe that the earth is sacred because it gives life. What is most important to them is not wealth or power, but rather shared responsibilities that show respect and love to the family, the village, and the earth itself.

Many of the Mayan villagers do not know Spanish, the official language of the country, because their communities have been cut off from the rest of the world for hundreds of years. The people in Rigoberta Menchú's village spoke Quiché. This helped to keep them connected to their ancient tra-

Who are the Maya?

The Maya are the indigenous people of Guatemala. In fact, within Guatemala, there are twenty-two different communities of people descended from the Maya, each with its own language. Like the Native Americans of North America, the Maya are often called "Indians" (in Spanish, *Indios*), because Christopher Columbus mistakenly gave this name to the native peoples of the Western Hemisphere. At the time he thought he was in the East Indies.

Long before any Europeans came to the Western Hemisphere, the Mayan people had built civilization that extended from what is now southern Mexico to Belize. They accomplished things that amaze scientists today. Without animals or carts, they built huge and complex astronomical observatories, temples, and pyramids out of stone. Before the Greeks or Romans, they invented a system of mathematics that included the number zero. They used their advanced mathematics to create a calendar more accurate than those used in Europe, and to make predictions about when eclipses of the sun and moon would occur.

The great cities of the Maya were destroyed when Europeans arrived in the Americas during the sixteenth century. Spanish soldiers and conquerors came seeking gold, wealth, and land. Their rifles, steel swords, and horses gave the invaders an overwhelming advantage in war. By the 1700s, most of the Maya had died in war or from the new diseases (such as smallpox, influenza, and bubonic plague) that the invaders unknowingly brought with them from Europe.

Despite all these disasters, the Maya and Mayan culture were not completely wiped out. Mayan customs and languages have survived in independent mountain villages like Chimel. For hundreds of years, Guatemala's rugged and beautiful landscape of steep mountains and canyons has preserved and protected these villages and let them keep their traditions and way of life.

As long as these villages remained independent this way of life could continue. But in recent times, this started to change. Roads and trucks made the land more accessible to the outside world. Wealthy landowners saw the rich mountain farmland and worked with the government to try to take it from the small village farmers. Today, most of the inhabitants of these traditional villages live in poverty and danger, and the Mayan culture is threatened with destruction.

This Mayan temple is found in Chichén Itzá, Mexico. The Mayan civilization reached from southern Mexico through northern Central America. The temples in Chichén Itzá are some of the few remaining. Without metal tools, beasts of burden, or even the wheel, the Maya built vast cities in the jungles with an amazing degree of architectural perfection. Around A.D. 900 the southern Maya began to abandon their cities—the reason remains a mystery to this day.

ditions, but it also separated them from the outside world and even from people in other villages, who spoke their own languages, including Cakchiquel, Mam, and Kekcho. The people who speak these languages are also descendants of the sons and daughters of the Maya.

When she was a young girl, Rigoberta did not know much about the ancient history of her people, or about the current changes that were threatening her village. But even so, she could sense that something was wrong in her world. "I hadn't had a childhood at all," she later said in her memoir. "I was never a child. I hadn't been to school, I hadn't had enough food to grow properly."

In 1966, when Rigoberta was seven years old, the Menchú family was in terrible trouble. They ran out of money. In the past, they had earned money by doing some temporary harvesting work in the *fincas*, the plantations down in the lowlands. But in this awful year, Rigoberta and all her brothers and sisters became sick at the same time. It was too dangerous to ask sick children to travel and work away from home on the *fincas*, and yet the family was in desperate need of money.

They had only one other choice. Rigoberta's father took the children up into the mountains to collect *mimbre*, a kind of willow used in baskets and furniture. Carpenters and furniture makers in Guatemala City paid money for *mimbre*, but gathering it was very hard work. Harvesters had to cut it from the trees, strip the bark off, tie bundles together with ropes, and pull it through the forest.

Rigoberta remembers what a difficult time they had. They had to travel deep into the mountains, often cutting their own paths with a machete (a long-bladed knife). After a few days their food supply was getting low. To help them find their way back, they brought a dog from the village. But they lacked food to keep him fed, so eventually the hungry guide dog returned to the village, leaving the family to wander, uncertain of where they were going. The rain forest was dense with vines, palms, flowering trees, and bushes. Often it was impossible to see more than a few feet in any direction. It was very easy to get lost.

It was hard for Rigoberta to keep up with her older brothers and sisters. At one point, she fell so far behind that she got separated from the group. She cried and shouted, but no one heard her. Her father tried to turn back and help her, but he couldn't find the path they had taken.

For nearly a whole day, Rigoberta was lost. It was a frightening experience for everyone, especially Rigoberta. When her brothers and sisters found her, they blamed her for failing to keep up with them. Maybe this wasn't fair, but it taught Rigoberta a lesson. From that day on, she understood that her family expected her to be responsible and look after herself like her older brothers and sisters did. It made no difference that she was only seven years old.

For three days, the family had nothing to eat but *bojones*, the edible shoots of palm trees. They grew hungry and weak. It was the rainy season and the sky was dark with clouds. When the *mimbre* got wet,

Why is Guatemala such a troubled country?

Today's problems are rooted in Guatemala's history. In the sixteenth century, conquistadors came from Spain, took over the land, and made the Mayan people work as slaves. For 300 years, Guatemala was a colony of Spain. Under colonialism, a more powerful country controls the economy, the government, and the people of a less powerful country. Guatemala became independent from Spain in 1821. Yet Guatemala remains a country divided in two.

A small group of ladinos (the descendants of the Spanish who conquered the Maya centuries ago) controls the army, police, government, banks, factories, and large businesses. The indigenous peoples (the descendants of the Maya) live in separate communities, speak their own languages, and work the land in a constant struggle for basic survival.

Although poverty is most severe among the Maya, many ladinos are poor as well. Currently, poverty affects nearly 90 percent of the populations and more than half the people in the country are considered "very poor."

The problem is that nearly all the farmland in the country is owned by a few people who run huge and valuable farms. In the 1980s, about fifty families had more than half the wealth of the entire country.

The problems of rural poverty in Guatemala are hard to solve, but the problems of the cities are in some ways even worse. Guatemala City contains more than a quarter of the country's population and more people come to it from the countryside every day. For a long time, the city has continued to grow in population, even without jobs or houses for the new people moving there.

While there are parts of the city that seem modern and wealthy, there are large and growing numbers of people who live there in terrible poverty. With no way to make a living, men, women, and children go through the city garbage dumps looking for things to eat or sell. Children grow up without hope. Because little else is available, many young people in the city turn to crime or drugs as a way to survive.

Poor people continue to be left out of the economic life of the country. Even when wealth comes to some parts of the country through exports, hotels, or banks, it makes no difference to millions of Guatemalans. For them, education, jobs, land, and money remain scarce, and they have little hope of a better future.

it became much heavier and harder to carry, and they had to take back much less than they had hoped.

After a total of eight days in the forest, they somehow found their way back to the village. They knew they were near the village when the guide dog came to meet them, barking and jumping and licking them, his tail wagging happily. The children were not happy to see the dog, they were simply frustrated and exhausted. This dog had been no help at all. It was a long time before Rigoberta could laugh at how they felt when they saw him.

For all their hard work, they hadn't earned very much money. It had taken the whole family a week to collect fifty quetzals worth of *mimbre*. That is less than ten dollars in U.S. money, but they wouldn't even get to keep all of it. From whatever they earned, they had to pay the costs of transporting the *mimbre* to the capital.

Rigoberta's father selected her to go to Guatemala City with him to sell the *mimbre* and conduct other business. Among other things, he planned to see government officials to help his neighbors claim their land. He wanted Rigoberta to see the world beyond their village so that one day she, too, could help her neighbors in this way. "When you're old enough, you must travel, you must go around the country. You know that you must do what I do," he said.

The great warmth and respect between Vicente Menchú and his daughter was mutual. He loved all his children, but he had a special fondness for Rigoberta, the sixth of his nine children.

When he would cut vines and brush with a machete to open a path into the mountains, he would invite her to go along, and she followed to see how he did it. On this visit to the city she followed him down another path and began to learn about his work as a representative of his village to the outside world.

It was exciting for Rigoberta to travel with her father and see new things. She had never been to a city before. In fact, the only times she had ever ridden in a vehicle were when she and her family rode in closed-off transport trucks which did not have windows. The view from the passenger window was something new and amazing to her.

As the truck passed through mile after mile of countryside, she couldn't stop staring. Brilliantly colored parrots, toucans, and other birds roosted in the dense vegetation and flew overhead, filling the air with their songs. Rivers rushed down the mountainside, cutting deep canyons. Banks of white clouds floated below them. As they bumped along, she saw spider monkeys swinging in the trees and beautiful flowers everywhere she looked.

She also saw villages very different from Chimel, with unique local styles of building. Cut into the hillsides on terraces were many tiny terraced farms where families tended sheep and grew crops. She saw families using machetes and long knives to chop weeds that grew around fields of corn, beans, and squash.

After the long drive, the capital was strange and overwhelming to her. She had never seen so much cement or so many people, wires, lights, windows, and tall buildings. And most confusing of all, she couldn't understand what anyone was saying because no one spoke Quiché. Instead, they all spoke Spanish.

Rigoberta's father had a number of things to do in the city. Wherever he went, he took Rigoberta with him and explained things to her. At one point, they

What makes Guatemala unique?

Guatemala is a small country about the size of the state of Ohio. It is located just below Mexico in Central America, the curving bridge of land that connects North and South America. Besides Mexico, its other neighbors include Belize, Honduras, and El Salvador.

Many people feel that it is one of the most beautiful places in the world. Concentrated in this small country are mountains, volcanoes, valleys, jungles, grasslands, and sea coast.

Though it is located near the equator, the mountain highlands are cool year-round, while the nearby low-lying areas are hot. Because of the diverse climate there are more types of plants and animals in Guatemala than any other place its size on earth.

Guatemala is home to pumas, ocelots, jaguars, tapirs, parrots, macaws, and crocodiles. However, because of deforestation, the cutting down of forests, many of Guatemala's animals are in danger of extinction. Guatemala has abundant vegetation: oak and pine forests; coffee plants; banana plants; and cocoa plants.

The altiplano, the highland area, is a kind of paradise. The soil is rich for growing crops like coffee, cotton, bananas, and sugar. Rain is abundant, and over 8,000 kinds of wild orchids and other flowers bloom constantly in the springlike temperatures which last throughout the year.

An active volcano looms over a low-lying area of Guatemala. There are numerous volcanoes throughout the Guatemalan mountain ranges, creating a constant threat of natural disaster.

23

went into a government office where they solve problems having to do with land. Because Vicente Menchú had taught himself some basic Spanish and had learned about the laws, the people of the village gave him the job of going to the city when there was a problem with land—when the government or a landowner tried to force someone to move.

Again, Rigoberta looked on with astonishment at something she had never seen before—a typewriter. She saw a man at a big table using this machine to fill a white piece of paper with writing and she could hardly believe her eyes. As they approached this man, Rigoberta's father took off his hat and gave the man a kind of bow.

Her father explained to Rigoberta that she had to be still and quiet in the office. These were important people who wouldn't let you talk to them unless you showed them respect. Rigoberta began to understand that the city was a foreign place filled with foreign people. They were ladinos—the Guatemalans who spoke Spanish. Many lived in big buildings and bought their clothes from stores rather than making them at home.

Despite its modern stores and busy streets (left), Guatemala City also is home to many poor families like those in downtown Guatemala City (right). Housing is a serious problem in this city with only 6,000 houses built each year and some 46,000 families left without homes.

During the three days that Rigoberta and her father did their errands in the capital, they saw mostly strangers; however, they stayed with a family that had once been their neighbors in Chimel. The family had moved to the capital, but were living in poverty at the edge of the city. In this area, few people had money to buy wood. Many families lived in shacks made from cardboard or whatever other discarded materials they could find in the trash.

The family was also hungry, so they had no food to share with Rigoberta and her father. Rigoberta was glad to see her old playmates but it made her sad to see them in the city. They missed the rivers, the animals, and the plants. She felt sorry for her friends. The city looked crowded and dirty and there was no place for a child to play. They asked her about the river and forest they had left behind with such a feeling of homesickness that it made her cry.

Before Rigoberta and her father returned to the village, they went to see the old man who usually bought *mimbre* from them. Though she couldn't

A man with three of his eight children in their home in Guatemala. The average number of children per family is five.

understand the conversation between her father and the carpenter, she could see clearly from her father's worried expression that something was wrong.

They moved on to see other men, but no one would buy the *mimbre*. Her father explained that the first man did not have enough money to pay them full price. Her father had tried to find other buyers, but he didn't know the city well enough to know where to find buyers who would give them the fifty quetzals they deserved.

He decided to accept twenty-five quetzals—only five U.S. dollars—from the old man. It was better than nothing, but would be a terrible disappointment for the family to have worked so hard and struggled so much to receive so little in return. At least the children were now healthy enough to go back to the *finca* and work again.

Rigoberta's experiences with gathering the *mimbre* and traveling with her father to the city helped prepare her for the responsibilities that lay ahead. In Rigoberta's village, all young children were given small tasks as early in life as possible so that they would learn the importance of work and responsibility.

The first job for young girls was usually carrying water from wells or rivers for drinking, cooking, and washing. It was a hard job because it required many trips carrying heavy buckets, sometimes for long distances. A typical first job for young boys was looking after and rounding up the village dogs, making sure they didn't wander off. Both boys and girls shared other chores, such as collecting wood for cooking fires and feeding the dogs, chickens, rabbits, and other animals.

Everyone in the family took the children's chores

seriously and treated the young workers with respect. Parents were very careful and patient in teaching children their jobs, but they could also be strict. If children failed to do their jobs, fathers would scold or punish them.

In this way, children got used to bearing responsibility within their families and community. This was the way the traditional Mayan values were carefully passed on from ancestors to parents to children. It was also the way that children learned to do their part to help their families in the struggle to survive.

According to the traditions of her people, Rigoberta was recognized as an adult on her tenth birthday. The Quiché and other Mayan peoples recognize tenth and twelfth birthdays as special community events to celebrate children's coming of age.

On Rigoberta's tenth birthday, she was finally told the exact date of her birth so that she could at last learn the identity of her *nahual*—the animal spirit which, according to Mayan beliefs, is assigned to each person at birth. They are similar to astrological signs. Parents keep their children's birth date and the identity of this animal secret until children reach the age of ten, when children can be trusted to know their *nahaul* without trying to imitate its personality instead of developing their own.

At this time, Rigoberta's family and the community held a formal ceremony to welcome her into adult life, advise her about what she could expect, and remind her of her responsibilities as a grown-up.

Each member of the family spoke to her. First, her parents thanked her for all the work and help she had given to the family. Then, her mother spoke to

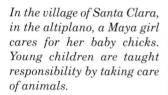

In the village of Santa Clara, in the altiplano, a Maya girl cares for her baby chicks. Young children are taught responsibility by taking care of animals.

her about what she could expect as she got older and ready one day to have her own children. She let Rigoberta know that she would be there to answer her questions, and be there with advice and support about what it was like to be a grown woman.

All her brothers and sisters, including her eldest sister, who was twenty-four years old, shared their experiences with her about growing up. Their stories helped her learn something about what she might expect as she became an adult.

Her father gave his advice: He told her that in their community, each person was an example to everyone else. There were rules of right and wrong passed down by parents from their parents. It was her job to follow these rules, so she could fulfill her duties to the community and contribute to the common good.

The ceremony ended with Rigoberta's promise to serve the community in exchange for being accepted into it. From that day on, her life changed. Her parents gave her two complete sets of adult clothes, including aprons, *cortes*, and *perrajes*, which are brightly colored cotton cloaks. She took on new responsibilities, and her family and the people in the village spoke to her not as a child, but as an adult.

Two years later, on her twelfth birthday, the community held another celebration. Traditionally, parents give children of this age animals to take care of, such as pigs, lambs, or chickens.

Rigoberta's parents gave her two chickens, a pig, and a lamb, and held a fiesta, a celebration, for her birthday. She took excellent care of her animals. After working all day, she'd come home in the evening, do house chores, and then spend an hour weaving. In about two weeks, she could weave three or four pieces of cloth, which she would sell to buy food for her animals. When the piglets grew big

A woman in the villiage of San Juan Atitlán uses a backstrap loom, the simplest type of loom, to weave cloth. Most Maya women learn to make their own clothing at a young age. The huipil *that a woman wears describes her cultural background, and social standing, and shows in which region she lives.*

enough, she sold them and used the money to buy cloth and thread to make her own clothes.

Rigoberta was proud of the ways in which she had learned to handle her responsibilities. But her father and mother had taught her that responsibility meant more than taking care of a few animals or a household. There were problems facing their village that no person or family could solve alone. Landowners wanted to throw the people of the village off their land and take it for themselves. As the years went on, these problems became too big to ignore. The Menchú family felt it was their responsibility to learn to organize the community and fight for their rights. Rigoberta was about to become a grown-up for real.

Chapter 3

SERVANT GIRL IN A STRANGE WORLD

Being accepted into the community as an adult gave Rigoberta great satisfaction. She was proud of her new responsibilities, which included teaching children, accompanying her father when he spoke with villagers about their concerns, and helping the other women of the village organize the community corn and bean fields—deciding what should be planted where, and when.

Rigoberta and her whole family were well-loved in Chimel. Juana Menchú, her mother, had learned traditional methods to heal people using plants and herbs. She was also a midwife; she assisted women in her village and others delivering their babies. In the highlands of Guatemala, there are few doctors or hospitals. Healers such as Rigoberta's mother were very important people. Rigoberta deeply respected both her parents, as did the entire community.

The Menchú family was always at the center of village life. They helped to organize traditional Mayan fiestas and celebrations at every opportunity. Rigoberta became not just the daughter of her family, but of the whole village. Neighbors freely shared their joys and sorrows with her and showed her great affection.

A young girl harvests coffee beans. Many indigenous children do not attend school because they must help their families earn money by working on fincas, *harvesting coffee beans, cotton, or sugar cane. Approximately 53 percent of the women in Guatemala over the age of fifteen cannot read due to their lack of education.*

This is not to say that life was always happy for Rigoberta and her family. Usually, they could stay in their village only four months out of the year. During the other eight months, the Menchús and most of the other families of Chimel and other altiplano villages had to go down to the coast and harvest coffee beans, cotton, and sugarcane in the *fincas*, the large plantations of the rich landowners.

Living conditions on the *fincas* were miserable. Families of workers, speaking a confusing mixture of languages, lived in one-room building that housed as many as 400 exhausted people. Arguments, crying

babies, and buzzing flies filled the air. Strangers slept crowded together side by side on floor mats.

Tragedies such as severe illness, accidents, and even death happened frequently on the *finca*. Children were hungry, and it was common for them to become seriously ill or even die from hunger or exposure to pesticides. Rigoberta's family knew this all too well from their sad firsthand experience. Her eldest brother, Felipe, had died after he was exposed to poison from working in a field that was sprayed with pesticides (farm chemicals that protect crops from insects, but can also harm human beings). Other children died of malnutrition—a condition caused by not having enough healthy food to eat.

As a young girl, Rigoberta grieved for these deaths along with her family. Her mother said there was nothing to do but go on living. They could not change the way their life was. It was difficult for Rigoberta to accept this, but she had been too young to defy or question her mother's beliefs or those of her community. When Rigoberta suffered the loss of her close friend Maria as a young adult, however, she refused to accept it quietly.

Maria and Rigoberta had been together constantly. They were both catechists (religious teachers in the Catholic church). On the *finca*, they worked side by side in the fields. Rigoberta delighted in Maria's sense of humor, as did most people that knew her.

One day, Maria was in a cotton field when, without warning, an airplane sprayed the field with pesticide. As happens all too often on the *fincas*, this led

How have old and new religions combined in modern Guatemala?

When the Spanish conquered Guatemala, they brought their Roman Catholic religion with them and they forced many Maya to convert. By 1980, about 80 percent of the Guatemalan population practiced Catholicism. But in Guatemala, indigenous people combined Mayan and Roman Catholic religions in a unique way.

In some forms of Guatemalan Catholicism, ancient Mayan gods are recognized. While people worship a supreme God, as well as Jesus and Mary, they also maintain some ancient rituals connected with a cloud god, a sun god, and the ancestral spirits of the village.

Each community has religious leaders who organize group worship. At different times in the year, communities hold religious fiestas, or celebrations. The community's religious system provides a way for men to gain leadership roles in villages as they carry out responsibilities such as organizing celebrations and serving as a kind of informal police department for minor disturbances during fiesta times.

The Catholic religion is powerful in Guatemala, but it also has had many enemies there. At times, bishops and priests have protested the government's harsh policies, which have hurt poor people. Because of the government's obvious neglect of its less fortunate citizens, many priests and nuns help the needy directly. For example, some poor children are given the opportunity to go to schools run by the Catholic church. In some ways, Catholicism in Guatemala serves as a voice for justice, although it generally focuses on charity rather than training or community development.

A Mayan priest performs a ceremony. While 80 percent of the Guatemalan population practices Catholicism, many indigenous people combine Catholicism with their Mayan beliefs.

to a human death. Maria was poisoned by the spray, and she soon died.

Rigoberta was torn apart by grief, and also by confusion. She felt love and loyalty to her family and to the ancient Mayan traditions, but she began to question whether she could continue to live and raise a family on the land, as her ancestors had, in conditions of such terrible suffering.

She remembered the times she would see her mother hiding her tears while mourning for her brothers. Juana continued to work hard and did not expect anyone to feel sorry for her. However, she had too much sorrow to keep all of it hidden, and Rigoberta knew how hard her mother's life really was.

Her mother's grief made Rigoberta afraid of having children of her own. Maria used to say she never wanted to get married because she couldn't stand to see her children suffer and die like so many Guatemalan children do. After Maria died, these words haunted Rigoberta.

When Rigoberta returned home to the altiplano, she told her mother what had happened to Maria. Her mother cried and then Rigoberta's own sadness and anger came pouring out. "Mother, I don't want to live. Why didn't I die when I was little? How can we go on living?" she cried.

Rigoberta's mother scolded her for saying these words, but Rigoberta meant what she said. She did not want to go on living this life. This did not mean she wanted to die. It only meant that she did not want to be trapped forever in a life like the one that had killed her best friend and her family members— a life of unbearable suffering. Her life would be different, she resolved.

Sadness helped Rigoberta decide that she had to separate from her community and their way of life, no matter what she had to sacrifice. Her decision meant that a part of her life would end, but a new part would soon begin.

Rigoberta had long wanted to learn to speak, read, and write Spanish, but the Menchús were unable to afford the cost of schooling. Very few families can afford to lose the income that children provide with their labor in the fields.

In her autobiography, Rigoberta relates that at first her father opposed her dreams to leave the village. Besides, he told her, he was suspicious of some kinds of schooling. Her cousins had gone to school and learned to read and write, but they had forgotten all the Mayan traditions they were taught by their parents and their community.

Rigoberta was insistent. She argued that her father had traveled beyond the village and learned to speak in Spanish to non-Mayan Guatemalans, but he was still loyal to the community. Also, she continued, he had told her that he hoped she could one day carry out his work. To do that, she would need to know how to talk to ladinos and understand their language. She felt sure that she was right, but she could see no way of meeting her goal.

For a little while, Rigoberta was given the opportunity to attend school. It was a private school affiliated with a convent of Catholic nuns from Belgium who had met Rigoberta's family. Impressed with Rigoberta's intelligence and energy, they offered her a place to stay in their convent and the opportunity to attend the school. This allowed her to obtain some

Why are so many Guatemalan children unable to go to school?

Guatemala has an illiteracy rate of 75 percent, and in the altiplano, only one person in ten knows how to read and write. There are a number of reasons for this.

Until very recently all schools held classes that were taught using the Spanish language, which few indigenous children from the altiplano knew how to speak. This discouraged many parents from sending their children to school at all. Parents in traditional communities were usually suspicious of schools because of a fear that their children would lose their Mayan heritage if they learned Spanish and the ways of the ladinos.

In addition, in many poor families every single person, including the youngest child, is needed to work and earn money to help put food on the table. Education is considered simply a luxury.

Finally, there are few schools in the highlands, and fewer school buses. In most cases walking to school is out of the question, because the schools are so far from many of the villages they serve.

For all these reasons, most children in the altiplano do not attend school at all, and nearly 75 percent of those who do drop out before the end of their sixth year.

In recent years, Guatemala has made some efforts to make education more available, but illiteracy remains a stubborn problem. As a consequence, only 150 out of the 25,000 students in Guatemalan higher education are indigenous people.

Children are packed into this truck which will take them to work in the cotton fields. If their families are to earn a meager four dollars a day, even the youngest members must work.

formal schooling. Rigoberta got another unexpected opportunity. A wealthy landowner invited her to come to the city and work as a maid for his family. He offered her a monthly salary of twenty quetzals, less than five U.S. dollars. Though this was not very much money, it was twice as much as she could make on the *fincas*. More importantly, it was a chance to learn Spanish.

Her father warned her that being a maid was a bad life and that rich people were cruel bosses. If the family had to suffer, he argued, it was better to suffer together. He was afraid that if she went outside the community and learned the language of the ladinos, she would turn her back on the Mayan traditions and never come back to the village.

Rigoberta understood how her father felt, but she had her own ideas. She believed this job would allow her to earn money and learn Spanish so that she could be a greater help to her family and her community. It was true that she would not want to be a maid

Women carry water through the streets of a Guatemalan city. Even in the cities, the only fresh water comes from streams or wells. Outside of the city, nearly 40 percent of the population does not have access to safe drinking water.

forever, but a young girl from the altiplano had few other opportunities to leave her village and make money. She knew that she wanted to escape the *finca* and travel in a bigger world. In 1971, at the age of twelve, according to her autobiography, Rigoberta left Chimel and became a maid in the capital.

Rigoberta had never seen a place as luxurious as the landowner's home in Guatemala City, with its floors and furniture and running water. It made Rigoberta feel out of place. She was not dressed for the city. Her clothes were worn and old, and she was barefoot. She had never worn shoes in the altiplano and had not brought any with her.

The landowner's wife was horrified by Rigoberta's bare feet and the one set of clothes she wore every day. The lady was ashamed to have visitors to the house who would see Rigoberta barefoot in her old *corte* and *huipil*. She purchased Rigoberta some dresses and shoes, but Rigoberta had to pay for them with her first two months of salary.

Along with one other maid, Rigoberta was expected to wash the clothes, change the beds, dust the furniture, clean the kitchen, clean the bathrooms, sweep the yard, water the plants, and run errands whenever she was asked.

Rigoberta immediately saw what little respect the landowner's wife had for her. It showed in many small but obvious ways. Rigoberta's bedroom turned out to be a place where trash was also stored. Her bed was a mat placed on the floor with no blanket. For dinner, she was given a few beans and some hard tortillas. Rigoberta couldn't help but notice that the family dog was given better food.

Rigoberta was astonished by the wealth of this family. Everything gleamed: their dishes, their windows, even the bathrooms. But for all this family's wealth, their behavior seemed strange to her, and they did not seem very happy.

In the morning, the father, the sons, and the daughter all took their breakfast in bed, calling, sometimes shouting, for Rigoberta and the other maid to bring them slippers, hot water, and more of their favorite foods.

The children changed their clothes several times a day and left them on the floor for Rigoberta to wash and iron. The landowner's wife constantly complained about everything. She complained about how tired she was, even though all she did was inspect the house and sleep. Rigoberta grew silently resentful. She imagined this woman trying to keep up with all her mother did. This demanding city woman would not have the strength to last five minutes in the mountains, thought Rigoberta.

At times, Rigoberta considered that taking this job might have been a terrible mistake. But whenever she had doubts, she reminded herself that she was only there to earn and save some money, improve her Spanish, and then return home to her village.

After eight months on the job, Rigoberta gradually decided that she had to leave and return to her village. Shortly after Christmas the landowner's wife gave her forty quetzals—two months of back wages. That money, plus the money Rigoberta had saved, would allow her mother to stay home and not have to work on the *finca* for a few months. These were modest savings, but at least it was something.

The landowner's wife begged Rigoberta not to leave them. She told her how fond they were of her and offered her a raise of one quetzal (twenty cents) more per month. Of course, this did nothing to change Rigoberta's mind. She set her date for leaving and began to look forward to being with her family once again.

What is life like for women in Guatemala?

In Guatemala, as in much of the world, few women hold positions of power in government or business. In most ladino households in Guatemala, the husband has traditionally been considered the head of the household. He makes the decisions for the rest of the family, and they are expected to obey him.

Women are also expected to obey their husbands and fathers in the Mayan tradition. However, women have tended to be more equal partners with men because the work they do for the family and the community's survival is often interchangeable.

In Mayan villages in modern Guatemala, men and women continue to do the same kinds of work. They grow food in their own gardens, and during harvest seasons, they do work-for-hire picking crops. Men, however, have additional job opportunities. They can join the military (where they can learn work skills), work in construction, or work in factories.

In the 1980s, the economic conditions were changing for the worse, so more women than ever before were forced to join the workforce. Other than farmwork, jobs for women have traditionally been lower paying. They include preparing food, sewing, and working as maids. According to estimates by UNICEF, most Guatemalan women work fifteen to sixteen hours a day, not only in paying jobs, but in unpaid labor such as housekeeping and childcare in their homes.

Because women are generally left out of the better-paying jobs, they are often dependent on men for their survival. This often gives men the power to treat their wives poorly; they know their wives can't afford to leave them or force them to act responsibly or fairly.

Because of all these factors, the conditions for women in Guatemala are as difficult as they are for women in many of the poorer countries of the world.

Indigenous workers eat dinner on a finca. *After working long hours in the hot sun, women have to prepare meals for their families at the camp.*

What is a political prisoner?

Sometimes unpopular governments will do anything they believe they have to in order to stay in power. This can mean using the army and police to jail or kill anyone who disagrees with them. A person who is put in jail for their opinions about the government is called a political prisoner. Political prisoners have been jailed for years or even decades, sometimes without even officially being accused of a crime.

In 1948, the United Nations drafted a document called "The Universal Declaration of Human Rights." It stated ideas that most nations of the world agreed were important for all governments to respect. These rules describe the conditions that every person in the world deserves to have. These include the right to a fair trial.

When governments act unfairly toward their people, concerned citizens in other countries have found ways to make their voices heard. An international organization called Human Rights Watch reports unjust treatment of citizens by governments. Another organization, Amnesty International, was created to put pressure on governments that unjustly jail and punish people for their opinions. Sometimes calling attention to injustice embarrasses a government that wants the world to think well of it. If many people around the world demand the release of a prisoner, there are times that a government would rather let the prisoner go than show that they are unfair or insensitive to human rights.

But unfortunately, the timing of this decision could not have been worse. On the day before she left, one of Rigoberta's brothers came to the house with terrible news. Their father had been sent to the prison in Santa Cruz del Quiché. Vicente Menchú had made some powerful people angry by helping the villagers of Chimel try to hold on to their land. Now he had been arrested, perhaps in an attempt to punish and silence him. The charge was very serious: "compromising the sovereignty and the well-being of the state." Lawyers told the family that he could be in prison for eighteen years or even longer. Rigoberta's father had become a political prisoner.

Rigoberta went to visit her father before she returned to work with her family in the *finca*. She was very worried about him. Prisons in Guatemala are among the worst in the world. Prisoners are mistreated by guards and their fellow inmates. They suffer disease and even death caused by filth and malnutrition. Many of the prisoners serve long sentences with no hope of getting out.

After she saw the conditions in the prison, Rigoberta worried for her father's life. The cells were dirty and flea-infested. Prisoners fought with each other constantly. They bit each other, they hit each other, and many of their faces were cut or bloodied. She heard men shouting in rage or from insanity. Rigoberta couldn't imagine how her father or anyone else could survive in such a place.

Her father told her not to worry about him. He had made a friend who was in charge of the prisoners' work. The friend had gotten her father a job making baskets, bags, and other items. This meant that her father was eating well and even making money to send to the family.

Rigoberta's father was brave, but the family was still very concerned. Through patience and sacrifice, the family was able to pay for lawyers and work with officials so that Vicente Menchú could be released from prison. However, this effort took more than a year.

In the meantime, life for the Menchú family had to change. Rigoberta's mother took a job as a maid in Santa Cruz del Quiché so that she could be nearer to her husband and help earn money to pay lawyers. The rest of the family, including Rigoberta, had to return to the *finca*. Rigoberta and her brothers remained at the *Pinea* and did not return until after their father came home.

At the same time, the people of Chimel were in danger of losing their homes and land. If they were going to survive they would also have to learn to work, plan, and make sacrifices together.

Chapter 4
LEARNING ABOUT SELF-DEFENSE

When Vicente Menchú went to prison in 1971, the people of Chimel suddenly had to learn to fight for their land without him. Unfortunately, this fight soon became much more bitter.

There was a long history to this struggle. When the Menchús and their neighbors had cleared a new piece of unclaimed land in the mountains years earlier, in 1960, it was not very valuable. It took years of hard work, patience, and faith to cultivate this land and make it productive.

When, after all this time, the land was finally ready to produce rich harvests, other landowners tried to take it away by claiming it belonged to them. In her autobiography, Rigoberta recalls that at first they appeared in the village and began to make measurements. Soon after, inspectors and officials from the government began to appear as well. This meant trouble. The landowners were trying to use the government to take the land away from the people of the village who had tended it.

For Rigoberta's village, the planting and cultivation of corn was a form of worship and a religious ceremony. According to ancient myths described in the *Popol Vuh*, after the Sun, called the "Heart of the Sky" by the Maya, created the earth, trees, mountains, sea, and sky, it created maize, or corn. Then, out of a paste of ground-up maize, it created the first people.

Rigoberta remembers how her family would burn candles in their house, praying for the earth's permission to grow the corn and beans in her soil. Everyone prayed to the earth, the moon, the sun, the animals, the water, and the seeds for them to join together and create food for the village.

On planting day, they held a fiesta and men, women, and children planted the seeds in the ground. The community decided together how the land would be shared. Common acreage was marked off for everyone to share so that whoever was unable to work because of sickness, injury, or old age would be guaranteed something to eat.

Everyone took turns guarding over the fields so that hungry animals did not dig up and eat the seedlings. Rigoberta remembers how she and her brothers and sisters would scare off the birds by shouting and throwing dirt whenever they came near the growing crops.

When it was time for the harvest, the village had a ceremony of thanks to the earth for its food. Together, women picked beans and men picked maize. The whole community celebrated with happiness and gratitude.

Land meant something different to the wealthy landowners. When they gobbled up the farmland in small village, they used i to make *fincas,* using farm machinery and chemical pesticides. These chemicals soaked into the ground, poisoned the wells, and made workers sick. The crops grown on a large *finca* were usually coffee and cotton, which would be exported to other countries. Crops sold abroad brought in more money than selling maize and other vegetables locally.

Why are the Maya sometimes called the "people of the corn"?

According to ancient Mayan myths, the world was created when the Heart of Heaven cried out, "Let the earth appear! Let the light come!" The mountains, the sea, and the trees emerged, but there were no people.

The Creators tried to make people from various substances. First they tried soil, but these people had no minds. The Creators destroyed them. They then tried to make people from wood, but these were too dry, stiff, and bloodless, so the Creators destroyed them too. It began to rain and yellow and white ears of corn grew. The Creators used the corn cobs and ground corn paste to make human beings.

The Maya valued corn as sacred. It was their main crop and they found ways to improve it through careful cultivation so that it could feed many people on less land. This helped make their civilization powerful. To this day, corn has special meaning to the descendants of the Maya because it has long been at the center of their lives and culture.

Creating a *finca* was a way to turn the earth into a big factory for making a lot of money for a few landowners, and a tiny bit of money for the hired workers. Unlike the maize and beans planted by the indigenous people, it did not give life, but mainly sickness and death.

The people of Chimel did not want to give up their land, but at first they did not know how to defend their right to keep it. Five years earlier, Rigoberta's father had thought that the village should do what the landowners were doing and talk to government officials. He led meetings in the village and gathered signatures to take to the officials.

Doing things legally, through petitions and land claims, did not work. In the history of Guatemala the right of indigenous people to their land was often ignored in favor of the claims of big businesses and wealthy families.

Rigoberta remembers when government officials told her father that the villagers could stay and grow what they wanted and that the land would belong to them. They asked him to sign a document. They said it would protect the people's right to keep their land.

Because his Spanish was limited, Vicente could not understand the complicated legal language in this document. He also could not afford a lawyer to read it for him. It turned out that the document actually signed the land rights over to the rich landowners. The people of the village had been tricked! The agreement said that the villagers would be able to stay on their land for two years but then it would not belong to them any more.

On a rainy day in 1967, landowners sent hired soldiers to try to throw the people of Chimel out of their houses. Many of these soldiers were poor Maya men recruited from other villages. In Guatemala, as in many poor countries, the army, police, and security forces offer some of the few possibilities for young men to escape poverty and have a job. These merce-

In the middle of a long day working in his cornfield, a campesino, a farmer, pauses to rest. Corn is not only an important crop for the Maya people, it is also a source of spirituality. The Maya believed that the corn god was responsible for the crops and the harvest. Statues show him wearing a headdress made from ears of corn.

naries (soldiers for hire) are hired to attack and intimidate their own people—people who are just as poor and desperate as their own families back home.

This hired army killed many animals in the village and then they went into the houses, stole whatever valuable things could be taken away, and smashed plates, cups, pots, and other household items. Rigoberta recalls that they stole precious silver necklaces which had been passed down to her mother from her grandmother.

The people of the village were shocked by the suddenness and cruelty of this attack. The murder of their dogs hurt them deeply. For the Maya, the life of a dog is regarded as sacred, just as a human life is. The soldiers knew this, and wanted to break the spirit of the villagers and make them give up their fight.

They did not give up, but they decided to leave their homes temporarily because they were afraid of being killed if they stayed. They quickly built temporary huts from leaves and plastic and housed themselves in nearby fields. Then, after forty days in the rain and mud, the community held a meeting. Rigoberta's father said that it was time to return to the village, even if it meant death. "Our people looked on my father as their own father," Rigoberta remembers, "and so we went back to our houses." They were able to live there in peace for a short time, but the battle was not over.

After the attack on the village, the people in the village began to think in a new way. They realized that taking petitions to the government was not going to protect them from the landowners. They had to be ready to organize themselves to fight back.

Why did Guatemalan soldiers attack their own people?

When there is injustice in a country's treatment of its people, governments often have to use violence to stop them from fighting for their rights. In the case of Guatemala, there has been terrible injustice for almost 500 years.

The indigenous people of Guatemala had their land taken away by Spanish conquerors, and since that time they have been forced to work on this land, first as slaves and later for inadequate wages, by Spanish landlords, and most recently by the Guatemalan army.

In the 1940s and 1950s, the Guatemalan government started to try to make laws that would help indigenous people get an education, higher wages, and a better life. President Jacobo Arbenz Guzmán had the government buy back some plots of land from landlords who weren't using them, and he redistributed the land to 500,000 poor people.

The powerful landowners of Guatemala opposed this redistribution of land. The United Fruit Company, a U.S. company that was Guatemala's largest landowner, also stood to lose a lot of money if Guatemala carried out this law. In 1954, the government was removed by force through a coup supported by the landowners and the Guatemalan and U.S. militaries. It was replaced by a new government, which was not interested in reforms to help the poor.

Various political changes have taken place since that time, but Guatemala has remained a violent and dangerous place for anyone questioning the government or trying to change laws to make life better for the poor. The army and the police, as well as "death squads" (secret groups directed to kill enemies of the government), were used to suppress any movements for change. They killed political leaders and even teachers and priests. In the 1970s and 1980s, after armed rebel groups began to fight back, this violence got even worse. Whole villages were destroyed, and thousands of people were killed.

Officially, this violence ended when the Guatemalan government and members of armed rebel groups who had fought against them signed a peace treaty in 1996.

Rigoberta's grandfather, her mother's father, lived to the age of 112, and he was very wise. He knew about history, and about the tricks that indigenous people used to fight the Spaniards long ago. His advice to the people of the village was to meet the attacks of the landowners with counterattacks. The people of Chimel respected his advice and followed it.

The community held another meeting. They decided that people had to live closer together so that neighbors could alert each other if soldiers came again. The land was redivided. The people of Chimel decided that the Menchú family would live in the center because Rigoberta's father was the village leader. Everyone agreed to leave their houses and move closer to the center of the village to support each other. As it turned out, they had begun these preparations just in time.

Within a few weeks, ninety soldiers arrived in the village and began to stay in the community house, which the villagers used for ceremonies, meetings, and celebrations. After dark, these soldiers went into the fields and cut down corn and beans, dug up potatoes, and ate whatever they liked.

This action showed deep and deliberate disrespect, not only because the food did not belong to them, but because Maya never harvest food from the fields without first performing a ceremony of thanksgiving. The people were angry, but they did not show their anger because the soldiers were armed. For two weeks, the soldiers remained in the village, and the villagers were careful not to provoke them.

One evening, Rigoberta's mother heard rustling in their field near their potato patch. At first she thought it was a neighbor's animal and she tried to

The United Fruit Company's banana growing plant. The United Fruit Company, an American company, was one of Guatemala's largest landowners.

chase it away by throwing sticks. It turned out to be a soldier stealing potatoes.

She became furious, and her anger made her bold. She ran out towards the soldier with a stick in her hand and several loudly barking dogs at her side and she began to shout at him. The young soldier was frightened and begged her not to hurt him.

"If you want to eat, why don't you go and work?" she said, her eyes blazing with anger. "You're protecting the rich and they don't even feed you." She threatened him again with her stick and demanded that he leave her potatoes alone. The soldier ran away, and by the next day, all ninety soldiers had left. They did not expect to find people who were prepared to defend themselves.

After this episode, the community made a decision. They agreed it was time to put aside their usual customs and traditions so they could concentrate on planning for survival and self-defense. At one point, they held a ceremony in which they prayed to their God to assist them and allow them to use things found in nature, such as stones, sticks, powdered quicklime, and water (which they boiled), to defend the village. They created a system of secret action signals and taught them to the children.

People felt they were in a life-or-death emergency, which demanded that they live and work together in a way they never had before. Nearby villages such as Chajul, Bebaj, and Cotzal had been attacked by soldiers and people had been killed. Chimel was determined to be ready if soldiers came. The whole village united to approve important ideas and decisions.

It took about three months, but people in the village worked together to build houses so that they could all live near one another. Using nets, they also built traps in ditches, on paths, and in all the houses to capture soldiers. They also made underground paths so that they could escape safely if the army arrived. Neighbors took turns keeping watch over the fields and the houses day and night. Everyone from the children to the elderly had special jobs to do. The villagers also practiced living in the forest so that they could stay alive if the army arrived and the people needed to escape for a few weeks at a time. It would be several years before the village's readiness to survive an army attack was tested.

At the same time, Rigoberta was shaping her own beliefs. Like many indigenous people in Guatemala, Rigoberta's religion was Catholic as well as Mayan. Her interpretation of the teachings and stories in the

New and Old Testaments of the Bible gave her courage to face danger and to help the village fight against invading soldiers.

Her idea of Christianity changed as a result of her experiences being part of a village under attack. She no longer thought that poor people were supposed to accept discrimination, poverty, sickness, and hunger as God's wish for them. They did not have to accept suffering all their lives and wait for a reward in heaven. In fact, the stories of the Bible gave examples of humble and poor people fighting against injustice for their survival.

She thought about the Bible story of David, the shepherd boy who defeated the giant, Goliath, with his slingshot; about Moses leading his people out of slavery; and about Judith, who fought for her people and killed a king. Rigoberta and other people in the village took encouragement from these stories when they had to learn to fight for themselves. Their Mayan

Soldiers stand in formation for an "Army Day" celebration. Rigoberta Menchù and her neighbors were surprisingly brave when a threatening troop like this one marched through their village.

The village of Chajul is located in the altiplano, the highlands of Guatemala.

and Christian faiths made them strong. This was fortunate, because when the soldiers did return, the people of the village would need to use all their strength, courage, and cleverness to meet that challenge. After returning home from Guatemala City, Rigoberta remembers taking an active role in the community's efforts. With her father still in jail, she was determined to carry on in accordance with his beliefs.

Rigoberta remembered the afternoon in 1972 when the army arrived in the village. People had been hard at work, building houses for their neighbors, when a child on lookout noticed two lead soldiers from an approaching army unit march into town. Quickly, the child ran to alert the rest of the community.

As they had planned, everyone in the village went into the forest and met in one spot. The child was able to collect a lot of information about the soldiers and the unit to which they belonged, such as what kind of weapons the soldiers had, how many of them there were, and how fast they were marching. The community considered this information and decided what they would do.

Rigoberta, her brothers, and some other neighbors volunteered to make a surprise attack. As Rigoberta's mother had done when she scared away the soldier, they wanted to show that they were organized and ready to fight. Rigoberta knew these armies of hired soldiers were not brave and only wanted to fight people who would not fight back. It was dangerous to attack a soldier, but it could be done.

The plan the community came up with was to wait for the whole army to come down the path and then ambush the last soldier in the line. A young girl volunteered to help. She offered to distract the soldier by trying to get him to stop and talk. Once he was separated from the group, villagers would capture him. Everyone had a different job: one person would scare him, another would trip him off balance, another would take his weapon.

Several hours later, the army marched by and the villagers put the plan into effect. The brave young girl went up to the soldier and began to speak with him. Without any fear, she started a conversation with him, asking him questions.

Suddenly, Rigoberta and an older woman from the village jumped onto the path in front of the soldier. Another neighbor snuck up behind him. They tripped the soldier, causing him to fall to the ground with his face down so he couldn't see. One of the neighbors shouted for the soldier to put his hands up and freeze. The neighbor was armed with nothing but his bravery and cleverness. Another neighbor told the soldier to drop his weapon. The villagers took away the soldier's grenades, pistol, rifle, and ammunition and led him into the mountains at gunpoint.

After the army had left the area, Rigoberta and the others who had taken part in the ambush blindfolded the soldier and returned with him to the village. When they arrived, everyone was excited and happy about what they had accomplished. Rigoberta recalled that she was so happy she was laughing. She could not believe that they had captured a soldier and his weapons without even knowing how to use a gun.

They took the soldier to the Menchú house. They got him to change out of his military uniform to disguise him in case another unit returned.

The people of the village did not want to hurt the soldier, but they did want to talk to him. The mothers of the village came together as a group and spoke to him. They knew that, like them, he was a descendant of the Maya, and that he understood their life. They gave him a message to take back to the other soldiers. They spoke to him as their own son. They reminded him how much hard work it is to raise a boy to adulthood. The ancestors and parents did not deserve to be betrayed by having their sons become soldiers who were enemies of their own people, they said.

The men of the village then came to speak to him and they told him to consider leaving the army. They told him that soldiers were not guilty, but the rich people who hired them to kill were. They told him that he could not find self-respect as a man by being a hired killer and destroying lives.

Everyone could see that the young man was very moved by these words. The village faced a hard decision. What should they do with the soldier? It was possible that if they released him, he might go on to tell others what he had learned. They knew this might be an important and powerful message to others in the army. On the other hand, his release might also mean danger to the whole community. No one knew what to expect. In the end, the village decided to let him go, understanding that this action might even cost them their lives.

This episode had a powerful effect on Rigoberta. After seeing the army come, she knew that it was not enough for Chimel to fight them alone. The indigenous people throughout the region had to learn what her neighbors had learned. Like her mother and her father, she had a sense of duty that was as powerful as her love of home and family. She felt that she had to leave her village and share her knowledge if their way of life was to survive.

Chapter 5

HARDSHIP, TRAGEDY, AND HOPE

From the time that Rigoberta's father was put in prison, everyone in the family learned to do a little bit more and work a little bit harder to ensure their survival. When he was released in 1972, they rejoiced. However, their hardship was to be relieved for only a very short time.

Three months after he was freed, Vicente Menchú was kidnapped. Perhaps angry landowners wanted to stop him from leading the people of the region to defend their right to be on their land. The hired men hurt him so severely that he almost died.

Villagers in Chimel found Rigoberta's father lying on the ground. They carried him to the medical clinic. When they arrived, doctors refused to treat him. The landowners may have given the doctors money to turn him away.

Rigoberta's mother had an ambulance take him to a hospital many miles away in Quiché. He had to remain in the hospital for over eight months. During that time, Rigoberta's mother once more took a job in town as a maid to help pay for his care.

This time, however, Rigoberta and her brothers and sisters refused to return to the *finca*. They vowed to stay on the land and grow their own food rather than work for the landowners ever again.

When Vicente returned home, he was still in pain from all the injuries he had suffered. His bones ached so much he could hardly sleep at night. Physically, he was never the same again, but his patient insistence on justice for his people never weakened. If anything, his harsh experiences made him more sure of their cause. He continued to help organize and educate people in the altiplano. Rigoberta and other members of her family did, too. They remained in the area, trying to survive as a family, but also working for a better future for themselves and their neighbors.

In 1977, Vicente Menchú was arrested again for his work helping people in the countryside to protect their land. Military officers came to the house, tied him up, beat him, and led him away. He was sentenced to life in prison, but this time the family was not alone. Vicente was well known as a good man. The work he had done to try to help the people of his village hold on to their land was written about in newspapers. It was a symbol of the unfair treatment that poor farmers suffered throughout Guatemala. Vicente Menchú's struggle and his name became known throughout the country. His fight for freedom was taken up by lawyers and journalists. Priests, nuns, students, factory workers, and farmers marched and chanted in the streets to show their support for him.

These protests made the judge see how potentially dangerous it would be to keep Vicente Menchú in prison. Fifteen days later, he was released, but the difficulty was not over. Government officials warned him that, if he continued his work, he or one of his children would certainly be killed by the same sort of people who had kidnapped him and left him for dead several years earlier.

This threat meant that he and the rest of the Menchú family would have to do their work in secret or risk death. They would have to keep moving from village to village along secret trails so the landowners would not know where they were. They could no longer live together as a family in one place.

In 1978, the children and their parents returned to Chimel and were able to be together as a family one last time. The neighbors were so happy to see the Menchú family after such a long time that they held a fiesta in their honor. Some of the neighbors planned to carry on the same fight. Everyone knew it might be the last time they were all together.

The fiesta was held in the meeting house. The village roasted a pig and ate meat, which is something only done on special occasions. Because of their modest incomes, poor people in the altiplano live on a diet that is almost entirely corn flour tortillas, beans, and rice. Having meat was a rare luxury.

These Maya girls are dressed for a fiesta in Quezaltenango. Celebrations in Rigoberta's village were just as festive as this one.

Near midnight, dancing and fireworks began. Then there were speeches. Vicente spoke, saying how proud he was to see how the children of the village had grown up to take their place as capable adults.

He told everyone that it was time for him to go on to help other villages, and that they should be ready to take care of each other in case he did not return. The Menchú family, their relatives, and their neighbors all cried, but it was also a happy occasion because they recognized that they had begun to learn to fight for their survival, and that in itself was a victory.

Rigoberta's mother then gave her good-bye to the village and to her family, and Rigoberta and each of her older brothers and sisters did the same. Their plan was to begin each in a different town. This was to make it harder for the army to find all of them.

Finally, Rigoberta's father said one last thing. He spoke to his own children and told them that the people they met and helped and worked with would be their parents from now on. He told his daughters that as women they should feel free to be independent and do what needed to be done. He gave them his permission to use their freedom to help teach others what they had been taught.

This was a very unusual thing for a Guatemalan father to say. Ancient traditions directed girls to obey their fathers until they were married and then to obey their husbands from the time of marriage onward. They were not expected to make decisions on their own, but to follow the decisions of father and husband .

Though Rigoberta's mother always put her family's needs alongside or ahead of her own, she also encouraged her daughters to see that being a woman did not require taking a quiet or passive role. She encouraged Rigoberta to use her skills however she could to make a difference for her people—to share her gifts with a world larger than just her husband and children.

With this encouragement, Rigoberta had begun to educate herself so that she could do this work better. Before her father had been arrested, she had traveled with him to meet the people he worked with so that she could carry on his work after he could no longer do it.

Eventually her father had realized that education could help Rigoberta better serve her people. It was not something that would make her just leave her traditions behind. With his approval, she got priests and nuns to teach her more Spanish; she also learned some Mam, Cakchiquel, and Tzutuhil so she could talk to Maya in other villages.

Rigoberta knew that even if the Menchú family never saw the changes for which they were fighting, other people would. This took away some of the sadness she felt. It was impossible, though, for anything to take it all away.

Rigoberta and her older brothers and sisters each adopted their father's work in a different way. Mostly, they traveled to different towns and stayed with poor families helping train and educate people about what the military was doing in the altiplano. They shared information with other villages about how to defend themselves. They also listened to sad stories and offered comfort to people who had lost family members in army attacks. They heard these stories all too often, and sadly, it didn't take long for them to experience this kind of painful family tragedy firsthand.

In a village in the altiplano, a family is forced to leave their home. Their entire village has been driven away by Mayan soldiers—like the one pictured in background—hired by the Guatemalan military.

Though the rest of the family was scattered across the countryside, sixteen-year-old Petrocinio, Rigoberta's younger brother, remained in the village. He traveled to different villages to do his work, but he lived in Chimel.

In her memoir, Rigoberta describes the events that took place on September 9, 1979, when five masked men attacked him, kicking and injuring him. They then kidnapped Petrocinio, and once they had taken him away from the village, they asked him where the rest of his family was. He didn't know, so he could not tell them.

Rigoberta recounts that the military wanted to scare people so that they did not organize themselves to defend their land. In her memoir she describes how they brought 500 soldiers to the village of Chajul and announced that they were holding a public meeting to punish those they had captured. They forced people out of their homes to witness the punishments.

According to Rigoberta, most of her family heard about this and came to the village to see if Petrocinio was there. Many men, women, and children had been captured and were going to be punished. The prisoners were brought in on trucks. To their horror, the family saw that Petrocinio was one of them.

Rigoberta recalls how the officer ordered the soldiers to kill the captured people, and they did. Everyone cried out in shock and grief. It was one of the most terrible moments of Rigoberta's life. Even years later, she said that she has to cry every time she tells the story. Rigoberta's mother was so overcome that she tried to run up to her son and throw her arms around him. Her

How are indigenous peoples fighting for their rights in Guatemala and around the world?

The indigenous people of Guatemala could never hope to escape poverty, have access to education, or control their own lands without changing government policies. Throughout its history, the government of Guatemala has opposed nearly all changes that benefited indigenous people. Until recently, it has been impossible to make these changes through democratic systems.

Because so few of the indigenous people have been able to read or write in Spanish, they have not been able to participate in elections or in debates concerning political issues. In addition, their low economic status has allowed Guatemala's leaders to ignore them in favor of wealthier and more educated citizens who do participate in elections.

Some indigenous people refused to let their problems be ignored. When a group called the Campesino Unity Committee took over the Spanish embassy in 1979, their intent was to alert journalists in Guatemala and the world about the problems of the poor people in Guatemala—problems that were not being reported by the government or by the media, which were controlled by wealthy people.

Respected international organizations, such as the United Nations, raise worldwide awareness of the internal problems within some countries and their governments' refusal to solve these problems. Thanks to the efforts of Rigoberta Menchú and others, the UN declared 1993 the International Year of the World's Indigenous People. Among other actions, it sponsored a forum that helped highlight problems of indigenous peoples in Guatemala, Ethiopia, Burma, Bosnia, and other nations. Such forums allow the international community to examine human rights abuses and influence nations, such as Guatemala, to change unfair policies. For example, international pressure helped bring about the end of the apartheid policies that harmed the majority of people in South Africa.

children had to hold her back so she didn't put herself in danger.

Rigoberta remembers that in their anger, the people watching almost attacked the soldiers. She saw many people shaking with rage. But the people were unarmed, and it was clear that the soldiers were willing to kill even children and old people, so they held themselves back.

According to Rigoberta's account, after the soldiers left, the village held a mass funeral for the twenty or so people who had been killed. Rigoberta and her family felt so much pain and sadness that they were unable to speak. It began to rain heavily, but nearly everyone in the village stayed outside in the rain by the graves throughout the day, out of respect for the dead.

After the funeral they all decided that the best way to honor Petrocinio's memory would be to leave and carry on their work. As dangerous as their work was, it was even more dangerous for the family to remain together for long. When they parted, they couldn't even tell each other where they were going because that information could endanger the others if one of them were to be captured.

Rigoberta watched her mother be brave. Her mother didn't want to make the neighbors lose their spirit, and she refused to cry in public. Rigoberta stayed by her mother's side for a week, until both of them were ready. Then she left home to travel to other villages. She felt more determined in her work than ever.

When Rigoberta's father was in prison, he had met a man who had an idea for a national organization that would help the *campesinos*, the farmers in the countryside. Later, this organization became known as the Campesino Unity Committee (CUC). Vicente Menchú was one of its founders and leaders.

Four months after Petrocinio's death, members of the CUC, including Rigoberta's father, risked their lives to call attention to how cruelly the army was treating people in villages like Chimel.

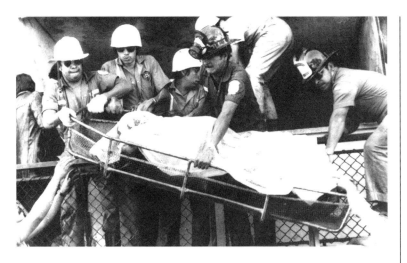

Red Cross workers remove the bodies of the thirty-nine people killed when Guatemalan police stormed the Spanish embassy, occupied by campesinos protesting their horrible treatment by the government. A fire started when a government agent threw explosives, killing most of the people in the embassy, including Vicente Menchú.

Because the government was censoring the news, blocking the public from hearing about army killings, the CUC forced their way into several radio stations and used them to broadcast information about what was happening. They also wanted to let people worldwide know what was occurring in Guatemala. A group of CUC members, including Rigoberta's father, went into the Spanish embassy in Guatemala City on January 31, 1980. They believed that the embassy was a safe place, and from there they hoped they could begin to tell their story to the world.

No one expected what happened next. A group of government agents threw explosives into the embassy and killed all thirty-nine people inside, including the protesters, embassy officials from Spain, and ordinary citizens. To this day no one has publicly admitted responsibility for this attack.

When she first heard of her father's death, Rigoberta felt lost. Since she had been a little girl, her father had always comforted her and protected her. When she had a stomachache, she would go to

How did Rigoberta cope with her losses?

In *I, Rigoberta Menchú*, a memoir published in 1984, Rigoberta described how she carried on after both her parents were killed:

All these memories are painful because those were very bitter times. Nevertheless, I knew I was a grown-up woman, a strong woman, who could face this situation. I told myself: "Rigoberta, you'll have to grow up a bit more." Of course my experience had been very painful, but I thought a lot about things, especially all the other orphaned children who couldn't speak and tell their story as I could. I tried to forget so many things, but at the same time, I had to face up to them as an adult, as a woman with a certain level of consciousness. I told myself that I wasn't the only orphan in Guatemala. There are many others, and it's not my grief alone, it's the grief of a whole people. It's the grief of a whole people, and all of us orphans who've been left must bear it.

Then afterwards, I had the opportunity of being with one of my little sisters. She told me that she was stronger than I was and had faced situations better, because there was one point when I was losing hope. I asked her: "How is it possible for our parents to be no longer with us? They never killed anyone, they never stole from their neighbors. And yet, this could happen to them." Thinking about this made my life very difficult and I often couldn't believe it or stand it. . . . Well, the meeting with my little sister was lovely. She was twelve years old. She said: "What has happened is a sign of victory. It gives us reason for fighting. We must behave like revolutionary women. A revolutionary isn't born out of something good," said my sister, "he is born out of wretchedness and bitterness. This just gives us one more reason. We have to fight without measuring our suffering, or what we experience, or thinking about the monstrous things we must bear in life." And she made me renew my commitment completely and showed me how cowardly I'd been in not accepting all this. This encouraged me a great deal.

From Rigoberta Menchú, *I, Rigoberta Menchú: An Indian Woman in Guatemala*, edited by Elisabeth Burgos-Debray (London: Verso, 1984), 236–37. Reprinted by permission of Verso.

him even before she would go to her mother. As she got older and faced adult problems, he was always able to offer her understanding and help her sort out her worries and ease her mind.

He used to say to her, "Don't be afraid, because this is our life . . . We must suffer it but we must also enjoy it." Rigoberta's father taught her many things; one of the most important was never to give in to despair or hatred, but to keep trying to make the world better. His death did not make her forget this.

The family suffered a second overwhelming loss less than three months later. Soldiers captured and killed Rigoberta's mother as she was returning from a trip to buy food for hungry villagers. The army had been threatening villagers for so long that some people were afraid to leave their houses even to get food. Juana refused to sit by while people starved. The soldiers who seized her demanded to know where her children were. She refused to tell them, even when they hurt her. Her love for her children was more powerful than her fear. She died to protect them.

In her sadness, Rigoberta recalled what her mother had given her and taught her. Juana had been a brave woman who showed Rigoberta that a woman's role was to care about her neighbors and family and to act with strength and independence in the world.

She had been a very practical person and knew how to serve others and be useful to her community. She traveled wherever she was needed to help pregnant women and the sick. When she worked on the *finca*, she used to wake hours before the sun rose to cook meals for the workers so they would stay

What are "human rights"?

Human rights are those rights that belong to all human beings. The right to life itself and the basic necessities of food and clothing are considered to be fundamental human rights. But the definition of human rights has broadened in the nineteenth and twentieth centuries. Human rights now make up three categories of rights for all people: individual rights, social rights, and collective rights.

Individual rights are the rights to life, liberty, privacy, the security of the individual, freedom of speech and press, freedom of worship, the right to own property, freedom from slavery, freedom from torture and unusual punishment, and similar rights, including those that are spelled out in the first ten amendments to the Constitution of the United States. Individual rights are based on the idea that the government should shield its citizens from any violations of these rights.

Social rights demand that governments provide such things as quality education, jobs, adequate medical care, housing, and other benefits. Basically, they call for a standard of living adequate for the health and well-being of the citizens of every nation.

Collective rights were spelled out in a document called the Universal Declaration of Human Rights, which was adopted by the General Assembly of the United Nations on December 10, 1948. This document proclaims the right of all human beings in the world to political, economic, social, and cultural self-determination; the right to peace; the right to live in a healthful and balanced environment; and the right to share in the earth's resources. The Universal Declaration of Human Rights also pledges the rights of life, liberty, and security of person—the basic individual human rights.

healthy. Her mother used to tell Rigoberta that it would be sad to die without ever having grasped the world in your hands.

Rigoberta's memories of the words and actions of her parents continued to guide her even after their deaths. She continued to do brave and remarkable things, just as they had taught her to do, though the danger she faced would soon be greater than ever.

Chapter 6
I, RIGOBERTA MENCHU

Work helped carry Rigoberta through the sadness she felt at the loss of her mother, father, and brother. There was a lot of work to do. Dramatic events were going on throughout Guatemala, and she was right in the middle of them.

Just before her mother's death, Rigoberta worked with the CUC to help organize and carry out actions that shut down sugar and cotton *fincas* and factories across the country for more than two weeks. Landowners had been paying their hired workers as little as seventy-five centavos a day, which was less than one U.S. dollar, for a long, hard day of work. Workers went on strike. They refused to work in order to make the owners pay attention to their request for fairer wages.

Before and during the strike, Rigoberta met with coffee and cotton pickers, factory workers, and villagers and taught them to be leaders like she was. She painted signs and banners protesting the landowners and she helped the CUC pass out leaflets so that other people would join and support the strike.

The strike was successful. More than 80,000 people supported it. To end the strike, the landowners agreed to guarantee the workers a little more than three quetzals (not even two U.S. dollars) per day. The government didn't like seeing the workers become so strong and united, so they sent the army and secret police throughout the country to hunt

What is a strike?

When workers have a complaint and want their employers to listen to them, sometimes it's simply too dangerous for them to do so as individuals. If a worker disagrees with an employer about what is fair, the employer may find it easier to fire that worker and hire another who is more agreeable.

For this reason, workers have formed unions, organizations that protect the worker by enabling them to decide together what they want to ask for in terms of pay, hours, working conditions, and other important concerns, and then present these requests to their employer as a group. If an employer refuses to accept the workers' requests, all the members of the union may vote to stop working at one time. This kind of work stoppage is called a strike. The goal of a strike is to make employers compromise with the workers and create an agreement that both sides can accept.

In Guatemala, it has been difficult to organize agricultural workers in the countryside because they speak different languages, and *finca* owners know that workers usually have to accept whatever job is available. It took a lot of work to educate and convince workers to support a strike. People need to be brave and determined to risk going without pay and making employers angry. And in Guatemala, workers who stand up for themselves often face violence as well. However, workers who exhibit this kind of solidarity, or togetherness, often succeed in building a better future for themselves and their families.

down the leaders, including Rigoberta, and to try to frighten everyone else.

During 1981 and 1982, the Guatemalan government used the army to kill, frighten, or drive away anyone they thought might disagree with them. They set crops on fire, shot guns into houses, and even bombed villages, including Chimel. Anyone even suspected of helping Rigoberta or other leaders was arrested and usually killed.

It soon became impossible for Rigoberta to appear anywhere in Guatemala. She had left the altiplano when she was well known as an activist and moved to the capital where she could be anonymous and safe. But many of the soldiers were boys she had worked with on the *finca* who were forced to go into the army. She knew that eventually someone would identify her.

Rigoberta left the capital and went to Huehuetenango (hway-hway-te-NAN-go), where friends provided her a safe place to stay. It was a difficult time. She was beginning to lose heart. She was sick with stomach ulcers and was beginning to wonder if she could continue.

In her memoir, Rigoberta explains that when things seemed at their worst, she received help from an unexpected source. One night, she says, her father appeared to her in a dream. He spoke to her directly and told her that she had to pick herself up and get on with life, that she should not feel sadness and despair for the losses she suffered.

When she awoke, Rigoberta's ulcers stopped hurting her; she felt cured and ready to go on. However, danger remained all around her. Later that day she was walking with a friend on the street and she realized that soldiers had recognized her. Rigoberta and her friend quickly darted into a church, and kneeled at the rail next to two other worshipers. To change her appearance, Rigoberta untied the scarf around her head and let her long hair down.

Rigoberta later remembered that when this was happening she was not afraid. She had no thought in her head other than that she wanted to live. There was so much more that she wanted to do with her life.

Soldiers followed them into the church and began to search everywhere. They walked right behind Rigoberta and her friend, but did not notice them, and passed through the church to go hunt for them in the market.

After this experience, Rigoberta took a job with some nuns as a maid and washerwoman in a church. She did not give her real name. No one had any idea who she was. This was good, because it meant that she could be safe; but it also was difficult, because it meant she could not talk freely to anyone. She had so much sadness, but she had to keep it to herself or she would be in danger.

After a few weeks, she discovered that a young man living in the church was working for the secret police. There was no time to waste. She had to leave immediately before he discovered who she was and turned her in.

It finally became clear to Rigoberta that she was not safe anywhere in Guatemala. She would have to leave the country. Her parents had taught her that her greatest responsibility was to be with her people and not abandon them. But staying in Guatemala meant death for her, which she was not ready to accept. The only way she could leave was by reminding herself that she would return. She knew that no matter where she had to travel, she would always return home.

Thanks to friends in church and political organizations, Rigoberta was able to travel secretly into the mountains and get on a plane that took her to Mexico. At first, she was a stranger there. Her new friends only knew that she was the daughter of Vicente Menchú, the Guatemalan national hero who had died in the Spanish embassy.

Living away from her home country was hard, but she soon found a purpose that gave her satisfaction.

What effect has civil war had on the people of Guatemala?

For at least 500 years, most of the people in Guatemala have been poor while a small number are extremely rich. The government that took power after the coup in 1954 stopped all efforts at reforms to help the poor people. In the following decade, people began banding together to fight back against the government. Some tried to protest government policies and organize workers. Others believed that the only way to fight the government's injustice and violence was with guns, and they formed armed rebel groups that battled with the army.

Fighting continued for over thirty years. The army fought fiercely against the rebels, and was brutal in its treatment of any citizen suspected of supporting them or of working for change. The government has admitted to destroying over 450 villages. Between 1954 and 1996, some experts estimate that as many as 110,000 people were killed in army attacks and that more than 500,000 people had to leave the country to save their lives—approximately 300,000 emigrating to the United States, and 200,000 to Mexico.

What these numbers don't reveal is how nightmarish it has been for the Guatemalan people to face so much violence and death for so long. While economic conditions are still difficult, at least for now, the war between Guatemala's army and its people has stopped.

In the village of Santiago Atitlán, people meet in the town square, as they do each December, to remember those killed by the army in 1990.

During an international religious conference, Rigoberta was invited to address the group about the lives of women in Guatemala. As she spoke of the courage and dignity of these women, her mother came strongly to mind. For Rigoberta, this was both sad and beautiful, and she spoke with so much love that it brought her mother alive for her listeners and for herself. Her clear, sincere, and honest way of speaking moved audiences deeply.

She soon developed a reputation as a powerful speaker. She received invitations to travel and speak all over Mexico, and even in the United States and in Europe. A man from the United States who had once worked with her described why she was so effective: "She looks at issues in a way that touches the everyday life of common people. . . . As soon as you see her, there's a feeling of warmth and a sense that she's focused on what's important. You know she's someone special."

Some villagers from Chimel look over what was once their home before an army unit bombed their village. Nearly ten years later, they returned to reclaim their land.

In her travels as a speaker, she was reunited by chance with two of her younger sisters, Luc and Anna. Though they were only young girls, they also had been doing important and brave work in Guatemala, though they had to stay in hiding when they were there. She was overjoyed to find out that they were still alive.

When she saw them, she was still in despair, wondering aloud how her parents could have been killed when they were such good and honest people. One of her sisters told her to take heart. "A better world is born out of bitter experiences," the young girl said. It was important to carry on without being defeated by the difficult things that happen along the way. Rigoberta was so proud of her young sisters. When she felt discouraged, the thought of her young sisters helped her go on.

In January 1982, Rigoberta went to Paris as a member of a delegation to an international conference. While she was there, friends who knew how powerful Rigoberta's words were arranged for her to tell her life story to a writer who would record the meetings and then make the tapes into a book.

The two women met every day for a week, from morning until late in the evening. Rigoberta told of her life in Guatemala, what she saw, what she felt, and how she had come to understand her experiences. Her spoken words were written out and turned into a book. *I, Rigoberta Menchú: An Indian Woman in Guatemala* was eventually read by millions of people. It was translated into twelve languages.

Rigoberta grew up with very little education and she spoke a language that few outside Guatemala could understand. Using the Spanish she had worked so hard to learn, she had broken through barriers that had kept her people from the outside world for over 500 years. Her book had made it possible for people who would never travel to Guatemala and could never understand Mayan languages to know, to learn from, and to care about the lives of her people.

She was aware that as she told her story, she was also speaking for millions of people who had lived and died without being able to tell theirs. Readers around the world knew this, and valued the book not only for its powerful and clearly expressed ideas, but for the way it allowed the modern world to begin to understand the sacred and ancient world of the Maya.

Rigoberta's voice again reached beyond Guatemala when she served as the narrator for a documentary film called *When the Mountains Tremble*, which showed what life was like for the people of the altiplano.

What is *testimonio*?

The book *I, Rigoberta Menchú: An Indian Woman in Guatemala* is an example of *testimonio*. It is the result of a Latin American literary tradition in which a surviving witness to hardship and suffering gives an account so that the collective story of his or her people, both living and dead, might survive. The opening paragraph of the memoir explains this tradition:

My name is Rigoberta Menchú. I am twenty-three years old. This is my testimony. I didn't learn it from a book and I didn't learn it alone. I'd like to stress that it's not only *my* life, it's also the testimony of my people. . . . The important thing is that what has happened to me has happened to many other people too: My story is the story of all poor Guatemalans. My personal experience is the reality of a whole people.

At this time, in the early 1980s, Rigoberta's own personal happiness was something she did not have time to consider. Her satisfaction in life came from her devotion to the cause of helping her people. Still, she sometimes longed for her own family, a home, and a partner with whom she could share her life.

At about this time, she had been engaged to marry someone she cared about very much. He lived in Guatemala City where he had a good job. His wish was to buy a house and live a comfortable life with her. This was what was most important to him. Rigoberta's strongest desire, however, was to be able to travel and live in the countryside and to help the people there. It was a hard decision for Rigoberta and the man she loved, but they decided to go on with their lives separately rather than give up their different dreams, which could not fit together.

Despite Rigoberta's growing international reputation, the Guatemalan military was still under orders to arrest or kill her. Even in Mexico City, she needed to travel with people who could protect her. Several times she had tried to go back to Guatemala, but each time, she was forced to return to Mexico because of death threats. Each time after she left, soldiers attacked her Guatemalan supporters.

The respect and attention Rigoberta was gaining around the world embarrassed the Guatemalan government. By telling the story of her life, she had shown how brutally and unfairly they were treating their people, and this made her their enemy.

Nevertheless, Rigoberta was determined to return. When the Guatemalan ambassador to the United Nations publicly invited her back in 1988, she used that gesture as a way to come home, with journalists from around the world watching to make sure that she was safe.

When Rigoberta's group arrived at the airport in Guatemala City, they were immediately arrested by 400 police, on direct orders from the Guatemalan president. They were pushed into a police car with darkened windows. Someone began taking pictures of them as they sat in the car.

Rigoberta knew that if she appeared fearful in these pictures, the government might use them to make people lose respect for her and the ideas she stood for. She wanted to look calm, so she reached into her purse for some chewing gum.

Instantly, police guns were pointed at her from every direction. She smiled at the policemen and they lowered their guns. Even though she had been afraid, she and a friend calmed each other by telling jokes. Not giving in to fear was a skill that Rigoberta had learned well. It was a useful one for her to have when returning to Guatemala, even for a short time. Rigoberta's visit was brief, but she did not let herself be intimidated.

The Guatemalan authorities did not want her in the country speaking her mind, but they did not dare harm her. If they did, they knew this would make them unpopular among the Guatemalan people and around the world. Rigoberta attracted attention wherever she went. The government couldn't afford to show that they were so cruel and unfair as to attack a woman who was simply calling for justice for her people.

Seven hours after she had arrived in Guatemala, Rigoberta and a colleague appeared before a Supreme Court judge. She was arrested on the charge of

During the national celebration of the 500th anniversary of Columbus' landing, Maya citizens responded with a large protest. Thousands of Maya gathered and chanted, "500 years later, the Mayas stand up." They demanded the land and political power they had been denied for so long.

encouraging others to commit violence. Telegrams of protest came in from all over the world from ordinary citizens and even from world leaders. It would have been embarrassing to Guatemala if they were seen to be this insensitive to world opinion. The judge dismissed the charges and let her go free.

Outside the El Dorado Hotel in Guatemala City, 1,500 university students and factory workers gathered to show their support for Rigoberta. Calmly she told reporters, broadcast journalists, and the world the story of what had happened to her father, mother, and brother. No one had ever criticized the Guatemalan government this way before: in public and live. It was a historic moment that opened the door to the possibility that freedom might return to Guatemala.

Still, the government fought back. Even though they did not harm Rigoberta directly, they punished people who helped and supported her. Rigoberta soon realized how dangerous her presence was to her friends. After her release, she decided to return to Mexico, where it was safe for her to speak out about Guatemala's problems, and work from there for solutions. For the time being, she would have to remain in exile.

Back in Mexico, Rigoberta kept up an active schedule of speaking and organizing. In one three-month period, she spoke to 310 groups. She had become so well known as a representative of Maya people in Guatemala that she was asked to travel to many countries, give interviews with reporters, and meet with government officials.

In her heart, what she wanted most was to be able to go back to her country and help her people. But the problems she faced on her previous trips to Guatemala told her that this was an impossible dream.

Everything changed one day in October of 1992—exactly 500 years after Columbus's arrival in the Americas signaled the start of an invasion that would nearly destroy the Maya. That day, an announcement came from Europe that would alter the course of history for Rigoberta Menchú and the people of Guatemala.

Chapter 7

A VICTORY IN THE STRUGGLE FOR PEACE

Rigoberta was in the Guatemalan town of San Marcos on one of her rare trips back to her home country when she received thrilling news from across the world. The Norwegian Nobel Committee had selected her from among a record 130 candidates to receive the 1992 Nobel Peace Prize.

This is a high public honor, recognized internationally. Since 1901, the Nobel Peace Prize has gone to courageous and inspiring people, from presidents to citizens, who have dedicated their lives to world peace and human rights.

Rigoberta's selection was a historic one for a number of reasons. At thirty-three years old, she was the youngest person ever chosen for the award. It was only the ninth time that a woman had been selected. But perhaps most significantly, she was the first person to represent the indigenous cultures that lived in the Americas before the arrival and conquests of the Europeans.

The indigenous people of Guatemala—who had grown accustomed to a seemingly endless history of poverty, unfair treatment, and even military attacks—saw Rigoberta's honor as an occasion for hope. As the world honored her, perhaps their government might begin to show respect for the Maya people, who had suffered in silence for so long.

What is the history of the Nobel Peace Prize?

The Nobel Prizes were established in 1901 by a very wealthy Swedish chemist and inventor named Alfred Nobel. When he died, he left most of his fortune as a fund from which annual prizes would be awarded to those who bestowed by their work "the greatest benefit on mankind." The prizes are awarded for physics, chemistry, physiology or medicine, economics, literature, and peace. They carry a cash award of about $1 million and bring international attention to the recipients' work.

The winner of the Nobel Peace Prize is chosen by the five-member selection committee appointed by Norway's parliament. Candidates are submitted by members in a number of international groups, including past and present members of the Nobel committee or the Norwegian parliament, different countries' national assemblies and governments, the International Courts of Justice and Arbitration, the International Peace Bureau, present university professors of law, political science, history, and philosophy, and past winners of the Nobel Peace Prize.

Once the names of the proposed candidates are submitted, the director of the Nobel Institute puts together a list of personal information about each candidate. (The average number of candidates is about 100.) At another committee meeting more information is required about candidates who have been nominated. It is up to the director and the advisers of the Nobel Institute to gather this material, often with assistance from the Institute's library (which is open to the public). Their findings are then forwarded to the committee members for consideration. After a series of meetings, the committee makes a final decision, usually in the first half of October, and the award is announced soon after. The presentation ceremony is held on December 10, because this date is the anniversary of Alfred Nobel's death. Ceremonies are held both in Stockholm, Sweden, and in Oslo, Norway. Recipients of the Nobel Prizes are known as Nobel laureates.

Some people in the government agreed. "From now on, Guatemala is not going to be the same," said Edmund Mulet, president of the National Congress. He told reporters that Rigoberta's honor was a historic event, and he predicted that it would change life in Guatemala in a dramatic way.

One of the first things Rigoberta said after the announcement was that she knew the award was not a personal honor for her individual accomplishments,

How many women have won the Nobel Peace Prize?

The first prizes designated in Alfred Nobel's will were for physics, chemistry, physiology or medicine, and literature. But a friend of Nobel's, peace activist Baroness Bertha von Suttner, had drawn his attention to the international movement against war that had been organized in the 1890s. Nobel had given the Baroness financial support for her peace activities. It was her work that influenced his decision to amend his will and add a peace prize to the other five prizes. He died soon after the second will was drawn up.

It seems apparent that by adding the prize for peace, Alfred Nobel thought that the Baroness would receive it. But four other recipients would have the honor before she finally received the prize in 1905. It took another twenty-six years before a second woman, Jane Addams, was given the prize, then fifteen more years until Emily Greene Balch shared the prize with John Mott of the YMCA in 1946. It wasn't until thirty years later that the next women, Betty Williams and Máiread Corrigan, were honored with the peace prize.

Since then the committee has honored Mother Teresa in 1979, Alva Myrdal in 1982, Aung San Suu Kyi in 1991, Rigoberta Menchú in 1992, and Jodi Williams in 1997. Yet of the ninety-seven Peace Prizes awarded since 1901, only ten have gone to women, even though numerous women have been nominated.

but a symbol that honored her people and their struggle for a better life. Within a few hours of the news, crowds of people began joyful celebrations everywhere, showing just how much they shared the feeling that Rigoberta's victory was theirs as well.

She acknowledged their happiness from the back of an open truck as they cheered, clapped, and waved handkerchiefs in the air. Everywhere, people could be heard chanting together, "Your struggle is our struggle!" and "Viva, Rigoberta!"

Thousands of people in hand-woven, richly colored clothes danced and marched in a procession. Many played traditional flutes, drums, and other instru-

A triumphant Rigoberta Menchú waves to her supporters during a parade through Guatemala City honoring her winning the Nobel Peace Prize.

ments. Often, Rigoberta's truck had to stop because of all the well-wishers who surrounded it to reach out to her and shake her hand or embrace her. At different points along the way, groups of Mayan priests and elders burned ceremonial incense making the air sweet with its fragrant smoke. Strings of fireworks popped loudly in celebration along the route.

Later in the day, Rigoberta took part in Mayan traditional ceremonies and dances. People representing different indigenous organizations honored her with formal gifts of fruits and vegetables from the earth.

Over the next few days, Rigoberta traveled to different villages in the highlands north of the capital, where villagers honored her with similar celebrations. No doubt many of those who celebrated with her knew her from working on the *fincas* with her and from receiving her family's help as they organized and taught throughout the altiplano.

Rigoberta was overwhelmed by many emotions. It was a time of a great shared public happiness and hope. But somehow she could not help feeling grief for those who weren't there to see it, including her parents and her brother. As she spoke to the crowd, in a hoarse and emotional voice, the many who had died were on her mind.

The eyes of the world were on Guatemala, she said. It was time for the people of this country, and for peoples of all races throughout the Americas, to forgive their differences and begin to live in cooperation so there would be no more killing. She wanted to dedicate the work ahead to the Guatemalans who had been killed, or who had "disappeared" after being captured by the military or police.

In their memory, Rigoberta told her listeners, "Let's give a cry for life. The disappeared will not die. They will be with us, and we will honor their names and their struggle."

Even after the long celebration, it was several days before Rigoberta had a moment to catch her breath. The announcement from Norway had brought the world to her door. Her friends and loved ones, journalists, world leaders, supporters in other countries, her allies from church and political groups, and even the president of Guatemala (who was more a political enemy than a friend), all wanted to congratulate her.

When she met with her friends and supporters, she was the same Rigoberta as always, a comfortable person who loved jokes and laughing. But when it was time to talk to reporters, she became serious and thoughtful, choosing her words with care as she answered questions about the future.

Overnight, she had become a world-renowned figure. Whatever she said, and wherever she went, her words were important for the causes she cared about. She had to be careful, because many powerful people strongly disagreed with her.

In addition to the honor that comes with the Nobel Prize, the people who are selected are given a large sum of money. The year Rigoberta was selected, she received $1.2 million. She was not interested in this money for herself. Her plan was to use it to establish an organization that would help promote education and basic rights for indigenous peoples in Guatemala and beyond.

Honoring her father's memory, she soon started an organization with offices in three places: in Mexico City, where she lived; in the United States; and in Guatemala City. It was begun with the goal of promoting peace, democracy, and human rights. It gave special attention to improving life for indigenous peoples, and for women, children, and youth in general.

One of the projects that the foundation sponsored was called the Summit of Indigenous Peoples. This was a special meeting of over 200 world leaders who talked about ways that the Maya and other peoples could improve their schools and health care, how they could preserve native customs, and how they could work with other communities to be treated with more respect and fairness.

To do this work, Rigoberta decided that she would try to live in Guatemala once again, even though the government had made this difficult for her in the past. Her desire to go back was not only work-related, but also personal. "Life is short," she told a journalist. She did not want to be a permanent traveler who never had a normal life. No matter what the difficulty, she wanted to be home.

What is PeaceJam doing to help kids?

The PeaceJam organization works to address the very real problems facing teenagers today by reaching out to young people worldwide with a message of hope for the future. Many teenagers are searching for meaning and integrity in a world that appears meaningless and unjust. They are looking for people to respect and learn from. PeaceJam tries to give teens the inspiration they need by connecting them with eight Nobel Peace Prize laureates: Aung San Suu Kyi, Nelson Mandela, Desmond Tutu, Rigoberta Menchú, the Dalai Lama, Oscar Arias Sánchez, Máiread Corrigan, and Betty Williams.

By celebrating the lives of these Nobel Peace Prize winners, PeaceJam presents positive role models of people who have lived their lives in accordance with the highest principles, working to affect change in their own countries and the world by fighting for freedom and democracy through nonviolent means.

PeaceJam sponsors conferences where young people have the opportunity to interact in person with the Nobel laureates. PeaceJam also offers free educational material to schools over the Internet, as well as educational videos and printed workbooks describing the lives of these Nobel Peace Prize winners and teaching how to use nonviolent ways to effect change.

The Guatemalan government did not share the joy of the majority of the Guatemalan people when Rigoberta won the award. The foreign minister, Gonzolo Menéndez Park, accused her of supporting rebels who used violence against the Guatemalan army. A representative of the army used words that were even harsher. He said, "She has only defamed the fatherland."

Rigoberta understood that there were always going to be people who criticized her, so she did not take this personally. "Perhaps I would have been offended once, but I now understand that one must respect people's opinions," she told a reporter. "Moreover, those criticisms are not personal but are addressed to an ideal that does not belong to me alone."

Her down-to-earth nature helped her in two ways. She could be forgiving of people who disagreed with her, and willing to understand their point of view.

Rigoberta returned from accepting the Nobel Peace Prize to thousands of supporters. Her receiving the award put Guatemala in the spotlight and focused the world's attention on the struggles of indigenous people.

She also could share her good fortune with others without feeling that she was better than anyone else. These qualities made her well-respected around the world, but especially at home in Guatemala. This respect helped make it safe for her to go home at last.

Once she was back home in Guatemala, Rigoberta was able to begin accomplishing important things right away. The government needed to show its people and the world that it was not ignoring serious problems.

For years, most of the people in the country, and nearly all of the indigenous people, suffered from poverty, hunger, and lack of necessities such as adequate food, clean water, education, medicine, and health care.

The main cause of these problems is that most of the land and the wealth in the country is controlled by just a few individuals. Rigoberta pointed out that

Temporary camps like this one were set up to accommodate the refugees like this boy who returned to Guatemala after the government agreed to redistribute land.

Here a class of school children poses for a class picture. These indigenous children are fortunate to have a school—children in nearby villages do not necessarily have this luxury, but the volunteer teachers pictured here are only able to hold class twice a week.

the way to start fixing these problem was for the government to give public lands to poor people so that they could have a place to live, grow crops, and feed themselves.

The government made a small but important step in January 1993, when they agreed to give land to 2,400 indigenous people who had earlier left the country to go to Mexico. Rigoberta was able to play a part in this.

A few months later, she was invited to serve on the committee that was suggesting candidates to run for president of the country. She was so respected that someone even suggested that Rigoberta be considered. The army is very powerful in Guatemala, however, and a number of high military officials considered her an enemy. For this reason, among others, her candidacy for the presidency was not discussed for very long. But it was a sign of how much had changed both in her life and in the country that she—a Mayan who grew up in poverty—was being given a significant role to play in important national decisions.

It is a credit to the work of Rigoberta and many others that Guatemala has finally begun to take steps to make life more fair for indigenous people. The government has started to provide public schooling in Mayan languages as well as Spanish, so indigenous children have the opportunity to learn in school.

Language barriers are also being crossed through writing. A new written alphabet for the Mayan languages promises to help the Mayan community develop one shared written language. This might mean the beginning of unity for the twenty-two indigenous groups who had been separate for centuries.

With improved communications, native peoples are getting involved in elections and looking to democracy as a way to help make changes in the country. Rigoberta has been very active in encouraging people to vote and to run for office as a way of improving life in Guatemala.

As native peoples become involved in politics, the government has shown interest in the issues that are important to them. In the last few years there has been talk in Guatemala about making land available to indigenous people so that they can live in the ancient ways according to their traditions. So far, there has been more discussion than action, but even this is a new and hopeful step.

Though these conditions are harsh, the situation is not hopeless. Rigoberta believes that the problems in the cities need to be fixed at their source. She has said that children begin to have problems when they are denied a normal life of home, regular meals, and education in one community. These are the things that the government needs to help all children to have. She also thinks they need programs that help them learn skills such as sewing clothes or making art or music.

There may be a long way to go, but Rigoberta believes that Guatemala has made great progress since the dark years of the 1970s and 1980s. "Our goals are ambitious, and it will be a long job," she has said, "but I think that it is primarily a question of education and information."

One other important role Rigoberta began to play was as a goodwill ambassador to the United Nations. Because of the work she did to promote the cause of rights for her people, the United Nations named the years 1994 to 2004 the International Decade of the Indigenous Peoples of the World.

Rigoberta has been an eyewitness to the darkest time in Guatemalan history and to its most hopeful chapter in over forty years.

She has suffered great and painful personal loss, but great triumph and joy as well on behalf of her people.

As it looks to the future, Guatemala still faces tremendous difficulties. Though a peace treaty officially ended the war between the army and the people within Guatemala in 1996, serious problems of poverty, hunger, and discrimination remain unsolved.

In the year A.D. 2012, the Mayan calendar reaches the end of a major cycle. Will this year mark the beginning of an era of hope and new possibility or a time of continued hardship? The vision that Rigoberta holds for her future and for her people may well provide a key to answering that question.

Chapter 8
LOOKING TO THE FUTURE

Rigoberta lost so much that was important to her, yet she did not allow herself to get trapped in feelings of hopelessness or defeat. She was able to hold on to her vision of a more fair and hopeful society. Having a vision of a better world and working to bring it about is what great leaders do, but it is also something that all people can do in their daily lives in many different ways.

"What I treasure most in life is being able to dream," she explained in her book *I, Rigoberta Menchú*. "During my most difficult moments and complex situations I have been able to dream of a more beautiful future."

President Jorge Serrano, shown here at an Army Day ceremony, rose to power in 1990 by promising an end to Guatemala's violent struggles. When his efforts failed, he fled the country.

Throughout her life, Rigoberta has had to call on her dreams to help her through difficult and painful times. Some of her most beautiful dreams have come to be: She has been able to come home to live in her country and help her people. She has also played a major part in helping to end over thirty years of destruction and fighting that had raged in Guatemala.

Like everyone, Rigoberta has also had more personal dreams for herself. Happily, some of these have come true for her as well. As a young girl, she wanted to learn to read, write, and speak Spanish to communicate with the world beyond her village. She did much more than learn a new language. She became a gifted speaker and writer whose voice has become a tool to change history.

Some of Rigoberta's dreams had to be put aside for a long time. During her years of greatest hardship, she decided that the happiness that comes with hav-

Guatemalan women hold a sign which reads "For the construction of peace and democracy—we are present at the peace signing." The Mayan people hope the peace agreement that the government signed on December 29, 1996, puts an end to the bloodshed of the past thirty-six years.

ing a home and children and a partner to raise them with was not for her. This made her very sad, but when she was traveling and working to bring peace to Guatemala she didn't think it would be fair to give so much to that struggle and also try to be a wife and mother. This was why she had decided against marriage, years earlier, to a man she loved.

Later, when things were calmer in Guatemala and in Rigoberta's life, her dreams of a marriage partnership and of motherhood, which had seemed impossible for so long, finally did come true. In 1994, she married Angel Canil. Together they have a young son, Mash Nahual J'a (whose name means "Spirit of Water"). They share a home in Guatemala City.

The story of Rigoberta's life raises many questions: How did one person manage to make a difference in a country with such serious problems? Where did she get her strength? How did she avoid becoming angry and hateful? What is her advice to young people who might see life as difficult or uncertain? Things she has written and said suggest some useful answers to these important questions.

Rigoberta has made sure in her life not to face problems alone. From the time she was young, she saw her father and her mother working with other people to solve problems that affected the whole community. Vicente Menchú knew that if his family did not join with others, that they had no hope of keeping their land. The family worked together, the community worked together, and eventually her family traveled to other communities to share their knowledge.

From her family and from her ancestors, Rigoberta learned that she was part of a community that was always with her. She knew that trying to solve problems alone only leads to frustration. She never forgot that when problems are solved by people who share the same ideals and goals, it is much easier to face difficulty together.

There have been times when Rigoberta was burning with anger, but she learned not to let anger take over completely. Instead of looking for revenge against enemies, she realized that what was important was protecting life, and helping people who had been denied basic things like food, land, and jobs, and the opportunity to learn, to be in a community, to be healthy, and to be secure—things that everyone deserves.

She decided that it was not right to try to hurt those who had hurt her family. What she wanted was an end to killing, not revenge. She and the people in her village learned to fight not to kill soldiers, but to make soldiers stay away.

Rigoberta believes that young people have the opportunity to discover "what we adults haven't been able to discover yet about humanity." She advises them to be creative and curious, and to explore life for themselves—not just to accept what others say about the way the world is, but challenge it to be better.

The message of Rigoberta Menchú's life is that the world can be changed. Courage, love, imagination, and responsibility are the tools that she used. They proved to be stronger than grief, or armies, or even death itself.

In the face of painful difficulties, Rigoberta has kept her spirit and her hope. Her words offer an invitation for others to keep their spirits as well. "I think everything that is interesting on the earth is also a part of happiness," she has said. "Not everything is lost. It is true that there is war and violence. The solution is energy, work, convictions, and giving of yourself with enthusiasm."

CHRONOLOGY

1959	Rigoberta Menchú Tum is born on January 9 in the village of Chimel in the mountains of north-west Guatemala.
1966	Rigoberta travels to Guatemala City for the first time with her father, Vicente Menchú.
1967	Rigoberta and her family pick coffee on a *finca,* where Rigoberta sees children die of malnutrition.
1969	Rigoberta is initiated into adulthood by her family and village.
1971	Rigoberta becomes a maid in Guatemala City. Vicente Menchú goes to prison for the first time. People of Chimel are expelled from their homes.
1972	Vicente Menchú is released from prison and then kidnapped and severely beaten.
1973	Rigoberta's best friend dies from exposure to pesticides on a *finca*. Rigoberta decides to devote her life to improving conditions for her people.
1979	Rigoberta's brother Petrocinio is captured and killed by the military.
1980	Vicente Menchú is killed in an army attack during a protest at the Spanish embassy. Rigoberta's mother, Juana Menchú Tum, is killed by the army.
1981	Rigoberta goes into hiding, then flees to Mexico.
1982	Rigoberta is invited to Europe as a representative of Guatemalan indigenous people. She dictates her autobiography, *I, Rigoberta Menchú*.

1988	Rigoberta returns to Guatemala, and is arrested. She is released after protests from around the world are sent to the Guatemalan government.
1992	Rigoberta Menchú is awarded the Nobel Peace Prize. She establishes the Rigoberta Menchú Tum Foundation with the prize money.
1993	Rigoberta becomes involved with the re-establishment of the Guatemalan government.
1994	Rigoberta serves as the United Nations goodwill ambassador for the Decade of the Indigenous Peoples of the World.
1996	Rigoberta assists in the negotiation of the peace treaty ending the Guatemalan civil conflict that had begun forty-two years earlier.

GLOSSARY

altiplano The Guatemalan highlands.

catechists Religious teachers in the Catholic church.

campesinos Farmers and farm workers who live in the countryside.

censor To examine in order to suppress or remove anything considered inappropriate or harmful.

colonialism The imposed political rule and control of one country over another, dependent country.

conquistadors Spanish soldiers who conquered native peoples in the Western Hemisphere.

coup A sudden overthrow of a government by a small group, such as members of a military.

extinction The dying-out of a species of living things.

exile A period of forced removal, such as banishment or expulsion, from one's country or home.

fincas Plantations controlled by landowners.

indigenous Referring to a tribe or group of people belonging to a particular part of the world who are native to that country.

ladinos The non-indigenous population of Guatemala.

mercenary A paid soldier who is not fighting to defend a homeland or belief.

nahual According to Mayan belief, the animal spirit assigned to human beings at birth.

ocote A small torch made from a burning pine branch.

perrajes Brightly colored cotton cloaks.

Popol Vuh The sacred book of the Mayas.

quetzals The monetary currency of Guatemala, named after a native bird with green plumage.

strike A work stoppage for the purpose of securing better working conditions for laborers.

union An organization representing workers in negotiations with their employers.

FURTHER READING

Books By and About Rigoberta Menchú

Brill, Marlene Targ. *Journey for Peace: The Story of Rigoberta Menchú*. New York: Lodestar Books, 1996.

Lazo, Caroline. *Rigoberta Menchú*. Peacemakers Series. New York: Dillon Press, 1994.

Menchú, Rigoberta. *I Rigoberta: An Indian Woman in Guatemala*. Edited by Elisabeth Burgos-Debray. New York: Verso, 1983.

Menchú, Rigoberta. *Crossing the Borders: An Autobiography*. Translated by Ann Wright. New York: Verso, 1998.

Shultze, Julie. *Rigoberta Menchú Tum: Champion of Human Rights*. Contemporary Profiles and Policy Series for the Younger Reader. Evanston, Ill.: Gordon Burke Publishers, 1997.

Books About Guatemala and Related Subjects

Brill, Marlene Targ and Henry R. Targ. *Enchantment of the World: Guatemala*. Chicago: Children's Press, 1993.

Cummins, Ronald. *Guatemala*. Festivals of the World Series. Milwaukee: Gareth Stevens, Inc., 1990.

Hadden, Gerald. *In Their Own Voices: Teenage Refugees from Guatemala Speak Out*. New York: Rosen Publishing, 1997.

Heptig, Vince. *A Mayan Struggle (La Lucha Maya): Portrait of a Guatemalan People in Danger*. Fort Worth: MayaMedia Publishing, 1997.

Montejo, Victor. *The Bird Who Cleans The World and Other Mayan Fables*. Willimantic, Conn.: Curbstone Press, 1991.

Montejo, Victor. *Popol Vuh: A Sacred Book of the Maya*. Translated by David Unger. Toronto: Groundwoood Books Ltd., 1999.

Palacios, Argentina. *The Hummingbird King: A Guatemalan Legend* Mahwah, N.J.: Troll Communications, 1993.

Perera, Victor. *Rites: A Guatemalan Boyhood*. San Francisco: Mercury House, 1994.

Perl, Lila. *Guatemala: Central America's Living Past*. New York:William Morrow and Company, 1982.

Rivera, Tomas. *And The Earth Did Not Devour Him* (Spanish and English). Translated by Evangelina Vigil-Pinon. Houston: Arte Publico Press, 1995.

Franklin, Kristine L., and Nancy McGirr. *Out of the Dump: Writings and Photographs by Children from Guatemala*. New York: Lothrop, Lee & Shepard Books, 1995.

Internet Sites

Rigoberta Menchú Tum Foundation Website: http://ourworld.compuserve.com/homepagesrmtp

PeaceJam Website:

http://www.peacejam.org

Amnesty International Website:

http://www.amnesty.org

Nobel Prize Website:

http://pl.nobel.se

Film/Video

Menchú, Rigoberta. *When the Mountains Tremble*. Directed by Pamela Yates and Thomas Sigel. 84 min. Skylight Pictures, Inc., 1983. Videocassette.

INDEX

Page numbers in *italics* indicate illustrations